THE NEANDERTHAL FACTOR

THE NEANDERTHAL FACTOR

A Murder Mystery

LAURIE ALLISON

iUniverse, Inc.
Bloomington

The Neanderthal Factor
A Murder Mystery

This is a work of fiction. All of the characters, names, incidents, organizations, and dialogue in this novel are either the products of the author's imagination or are used fictitiously.

iUniverse books may be ordered through booksellers or by contacting:

iUniverse
1663 Liberty Drive
Bloomington, IN 47403
www.iuniverse.com
1-800-Authors (1-800-288-4677)

ISBN: 978-1-4759-4484-6 (sc)
ISBN: 978-1-4759-4485-3 (hc)
ISBN: 978-1-4759-4486-0 (e)

Library of Congress Control Number: 2012914930

Printed in the United States of America

iUniverse rev. date: 09/25/2012

From the *New York Post*, September 2, 2006
MCMANUS THROWS HIS HAT IN THE RING

Last evening, James McManus, New York City's flamboyant mayor, called a press conference at Gracie Mansion and officially declared his intention to run for president of the United States.

From the *New York Times*, September 2, 2006
GREAT SILK ROAD EXHIBITION SIGNALS INTERNATIONAL COOPERATION

New York's Metropolitan Museum of Art and the Wyndham Institute of Art and Culture have announced plans for a joint exhibition on the Great Silk Road, the major trade route linking East and West in the ancient and medieval worlds. The exhibition will be cosponsored by the Egyptian, Israeli, and Chinese governments and will feature significant objects from their national museums. This event will be a milestone in international cultural cooperation. A gala dinner will be held in the auditorium of the Wyndham Institute on the evening preceding the opening, and Mayor McManus will act as host.

From the *London Financial Times*, September 2, 2006
DESPITE US EFFORT, OPIUM PRODUCTION ON THE RISE IN AFGHANISTAN

From the *New York Sun*, September 2, 2006
BOMB DEMOLISHES SYNAGOGUE IN BROOKLYN. TWELVE KNOWN DEAD.

From the *International Herald Tribune*, September 2, 2006
STOLEN OBJECTS FOUND AT HOTEL DRUOUT

According to Interpol, several gold objects looted from excavations on the Aegean island of Santorini were up for auction at the Hôtel Druout in Paris yesterday. The Greek government is demanding their return.

From the *Bogotá Courier*, September 2, 2006

DRUG WAR ESCALATES

Twelve policemen were shot and killed in an early morning drug raid in Cali, Colombia. Authorities confiscated over two tons of cocaine. Documents seized by police confirm that the drugs were bound for New York City.

From the *Hong Kong Herald*, September 2, 2006

CHINESE DEMAND INVESTIGATION

Hong Kong police have discovered a smuggling operation involving ancient works of art from mainland China. An anonymous tip led investigators to a warehouse in eastern Kowloon, where Bronze Age objects were packed for shipment to the United States. The Chinese government is demanding an investigation.

From the *New York Sun*, September 2, 2006

THE NEW YORK SCENE

Who was that shapely brunette dining with New York's most eligible bachelor, Ricardo Guzman Montoya, curator of pre-Colombian art at the prestigious Wyndham Institute of Art and Culture? Montoya isn't talking. Perhaps a buttoned lip is the best policy in view of the rumors circulating about problems at the Institute.

CHAPTER 1

Wednesday, September 2, 2006, 6:30 p.m.

With a detective's nose for trouble, Joseph Padrone knew that something was wrong. He kicked open the door to Nick's office and was blinded by a bombardment of bright lights blinking on and off at high speed. Between each blast of light, Padrone heard a click and blinked in response. He whirled around toward the source of the lights and saw one pair of images after another flash in rapid succession on the wall.

"Slide projectors," Padrone muttered. "They've gone wild!" He felt for the light switch.

The office was bathed in light. The antiquated carousels continued to turn. Then Padrone saw the figure.

Samuel Wyndham was slumped over Nick's desk. Blood poured from a deep gash that had nearly severed his neck. The red stream oozed across the desk, running over its edge and down onto the floor. Wyndham's head was turned away from the slide projector, toward the office door. His glasses hung sideways from his left ear, swaying slightly. Wyndham's face was like a mask—his eyes staring, his mouth set in a grimace.

Padrone detected no signs of a struggle.

The clicking continued. Padrone saw that Wyndham's left hand still gripped the remote control that set the images in motion. Even in death he was running the show, Padrone thought to himself as he switched off the projectors. Padrone put on the pair of rubber gloves he always carried in his pocket to make sure any fingerprints would not be damaged.

To Padrone's astonishment, Wyndham was not alone. His protégé, Nicholas d'Abernon, stood directly behind him. His back was to the open door of the darkroom behind the desk. The red safelight was still on. Nick seemed unsure of where he was or of what he was doing. Padrone saw that he was holding a bronze, double-headed ax. It was dripping with blood.

Padrone drew his revolver and pointed it directly at Nick. "Don't move, d'Abernon! Stay right where you are!"

Nick froze.

Padrone flicked on his walkie-talkie and sent out a call for security.

CHAPTER 2

Monday, November 15, 2006, 10:45 a.m.
Criminal Court, New York, New York

"Nicholas d'Abernon, you have been charged with the premeditated murder of Samuel Wyndham on the evening of September 2. How do you plead?"

"Not guilty, Your Honor."

CHAPTER 3

Wednesday, November 17, 10:00 a.m.

The indictment of murder in the first degree still rang in Nick's ears. At the arraignment he had been dimly aware of the crowd in the courtroom, the commotion outside, and the barrage of reporters' questions and flashbulbs as spectators pushed through the heavy wooden doors. Now, with the trial in session, the sound of the gavel brought Nick back to reality. He knew he was on trial for his life. The wheels of justice had been set in motion.

Nick felt as if he were a spectator observing his own fate. He was becoming ever more deeply enmeshed in events beyond his control. First the indictment for murder, then the selection of a jury—eight men and four women—and now the trial. It had all happened so fast. Images flashed through Nick's mind: He stood over Samuel Wyndham with a bronze Minoan ax in his hand. Blood was everywhere. Padrone kicked in the door. He was arrested.

Nick knew that the case had become a political football. How else could it have gotten on the court docket so quickly? Someone had managed to push up the case on the court calendar. But who? he wondered. And why?

Samuel Wyndham's lurid murder had been described in the press as the act of a vicious killer, and Nick was being held without bail. His lawyer, Chris Rogers, had urged him to plead temporary insanity, but Nick refused. And he had finally persuaded Rogers that he was rational—if not innocent.

Nick worried about his professional future and his future with Ruth, his fiancée and Samuel Wyndham's only daughter. All was a kaleidoscopic jumble that Nick was unable to arrange into a coherent picture. And he had lost track of time. How long, he wondered, had it been since he first saw Samuel's grotesque figure slumped over the desk? The image of Samuel's nearly severed neck and the ax dripping with blood haunted his dreams.

One thing was clear to Nick: the odds were not in his favor. The district attorney's opening statement to the jury was a vigorous condemnation. Nick thought it was amazing how well the district attorney could manipulate language for effect, the effect of establishing his guilt.

"And I will show that Nicholas d'Abernon had motive and opportunity for savagely murdering the man who had entrusted him with the future of one of the most famous research institutions in the world. That Nicholas d'Abernon, by his brutal act, has deprived civilization of one of its greatest benefactors."

Forty-six-year-old Sinclair Crawford III, the Manhattan district attorney, seemed to Nick to tip the proverbial scales of justice. Crawford was a golden boy of New York politics, slated in the eyes of many for higher office. His father, a former president of the New York Bar Association, was rumored to be short-listed to fill a recent vacancy on the Supreme Court. He was the senior partner of Crawford, Collins, and Dunbar, one of the city's oldest white-shoe law firms. Everyone knew that his son, Sinclair Crawford III, considered his present job a steppingstone to a seat in the United States Senate. Some journalists had referred to him as future presidential material. Nick realized that the sensationalism of this trial, enhanced by Wyndham's fame, was a showcase for Crawford's political ambitions.

"And furthermore, ladies and gentlemen of the jury, I will produce witnesses who will testify that Nicholas d'Abernon was driven by ambition when he deprived Samuel Wyndham of his life. Ambition and fear, ladies and gentlemen. In the course of this trial, you will hear that he argued with Samuel Wyndham and that Samuel Wyndham threatened to ruin his career. It is common knowledge that Samuel Wyndham had appointed the defendant to succeed him as director of the Wyndham Institute of Art and Culture, an appointment of enormous prestige and power. *And* potential wealth. Not an appointment to be taken lightly. Nicholas d'Abernon did not take it lightly. I will show, beyond the shadow of a doubt, just how seriously he took Samuel Wyndham's threat, even to the point of committing murder. The murder of a world-renowned scientist—a man who discovered one of the most significant missing links of human evolution: *Homo jekyllensis.*

"In brutally murdering Samuel Wyndham, Nicholas d'Abernon deprived civilization of one of its brightest lights. His murder is a great loss to his family, our great city, and the international community."

He certainly is good, Nick thought. By comparison with his own lawyer, plain old Chris Rogers from Brooklyn, Sinclair Crawford III was a sure winner, a natural prosecutor, who relished his job and could sway a jury with the power of his rhetoric. He was one of the old guard by birth, silver spoon and all. You needed money for lawyers like Crawford, and Nick had refused to accept a cent from Ruth.

Nick glanced at Rogers as he shuffled a stack of papers. He was acutely aware of the social gap separating his lawyer from the prosecuting attorney. Sure, Chris Rogers would do his best. He was earnest and thorough, although plodding seemed a better term to Nick at the moment. No brilliance or flair. No natural self-confidence. No silver spoon. Nick could see it in their clothes, in their posture, and their gestures said it all. The jury sensed it too, particularly the foreman, a stocky, middle-aged man whose attention wandered whenever Rogers rose to speak.

Crawford was self-confident. Rogers was hesitant. Rogers wore thick horn-rimmed glasses, which were too big for his narrow face and small nose. He squinted as if he needed a stronger prescription. He tried to look like a lawyer, but he didn't have it in him. His dark-blue suit was not cut with the same smooth perfection as Crawford's charcoal-gray Armani suit. Crawford's pale-blue shirt, elegant but subdued blue-and-gray Hermes tie, and black wingtip shoes made Roger's short-sleeved white shirt and narrow black tie stand out all the more. Rogers reminded Nick of an accountant. His socks slipped when he crossed his legs, revealing pale skin between the top of his socks and his trouser cuffs.

Crawford's socks never slipped. He probably keeps them up with little suspenders, Nick thought. His French cuffs were fastened with tasteful, gold cufflinks. To make matters worse, this was Rogers's first murder trial. He had not been out of law school more than a few years. And he had not attended Yale, as Crawford had, but earned his degree at night after a full day of working as a high-school math teacher. Nick knew that Rogers would do his best, but when even your own lawyer is not convinced of your innocence, how can you expect him to persuade the jury? And Ruth? How long would she continue to believe in him?

Nick turned around toward the spectators and caught Ruth's eye. She sat on the aisle at the back of the courtroom. He wished he could take her in his arms and explain again why he refused to let her pay for his defense. It was a matter of pride. Their eyes met. Ruth smiled encouragingly. Nick realized that for her this was a double blow. First her father's gruesome death and then her fiancé's arrest for his murder. And Nick knew that Joe Padrone, who had always been protective of Ruth, would do his best to turn her against him.

"And finally," concluded Sinclair Crawford III, "the prosecution will demonstrate that Nicholas d'Abernon was motivated not only by fear and ambition but also by opportunism. Yes, ladies and gentlemen, he was engaged to marry Ruth Wyndham, Samuel Wyndham's daughter and sole heir, thereby planning to cement his hold on the Institute." Crawford paused. "And on Samuel Wyndham's considerable fortune ..."

Nick started to protest, but his lawyer restrained him. "Take it easy," Rogers cautioned. "It's all part of the performance."

Nick controlled his anger with difficulty. He did not trust himself to turn around and glance at Ruth a second time.

When Chris Rogers rose to make his opening statement for the defense, Nick's heart sank. Rogers kept looking at his notes and pausing in the middle of sentences. He was losing the jury. When Crawford spoke, all twelve jurors paid attention. When Rogers addressed the jury, Nick counted four yawns in the front row. Even the judge's attention seemed to wander. He was in his early sixties and known to be hard on violent crime and impatient with inexperienced lawyers.

Nick had reservations about Rogers's strategy. His decision not to put Nick on the stand suggested that he had no confidence in his client. Nick thought surely his attitude would be evident to the jury.

"And the defense will show that the prosecution does not have an open-and-shut case. In fact, there is a great deal of doubt about what actually happened the night of Samuel Wyndham's death. My client was indeed present at the scene of the crime. It took place in his office. But a man is expected to be in his office during working hours."

Terrific, thought Nick. What about the ax, you idiot? Was he expected to be handling an ax dripping with blood not two feet from the murdered man? Maybe he *would* be a bad witness. Maybe Rogers was right. Nick was relieved when Rogers sat down.

There was a rustle in the courtroom as the prosecution prepared to call its first witness.

The phone rang in the district attorney's office. One of Crawford's assistants answered.

"How's it looking?" asked the familiar voice of a deputy mayor.

"Take it easy. The trial is just beginning. We got it moved up on the calendar and persuaded the judge to deny bail. One thing at a time."

"We need a quick conviction." The voice was urgent. "No slip-ups. A lot is riding on this and security is a problem."

"I know. And I don't suppose the political implications are of any concern to his honor, the mayor." The sarcasm was unmistakable.

"I've been instructed to tell you to make sure that Crawford gets the message. His career is riding on this case."

"I can't tell Crawford anything at the moment. He's about to call his first witness.

CHAPTER 4

Wednesday, November 17, 2:00 p.m.

The first witness for the prosecution was a forensic scientist, James Williams, a tall man in his fifties with graying hair. He wore a rumpled brown suit, a creased white shirt, and a brown-and-white striped tie. He looked as if he had been up all night. His testimony, a macabre prologue to the unfolding of the trial, was delivered in a monotone. But even his monotonous tone did nothing to diminish his vivid description of Samuel Wyndham's violent death.

Wyndham, Williams testified, was struck on the left side of his neck with unusual force. The double-headed bronze ax in Nick's hands was, in fact, the murder weapon. The blood on it matched Samuel Wyndham's and the fingerprints were Nick's. Wyndham had been dead a very short time, a matter of minutes, when Padrone found him. The prosecutor made a point of the blow being on the left side, and the forensic scientist confirmed that if Wyndham had been struck from behind, the murderer would have to have been left-handed.

"Objection!" Rogers jumped up. "No evidence has been offered to suggest that Wyndham was hit from behind."

"D'Abernon is left-handed. *And* he was behind Wyndham when Joseph Padrone entered the office," Crawford retorted quickly.

There was an uproar in the courtroom.

"Your Honor, I must object again," Rogers insisted. "My client has not yet been found guilty."

"Sustained," agreed the judge.

Nick froze at the implied allegation. He *was* left-handed. Not only that, he was a regular squash player and his left arm was strong.

On cross-examination Rogers had only one question: "Could the blow have been struck by a right-handed person from the front?"

"It's possible," replied Williams without much conviction.

CHAPTER 5

Thursday, November 18, 10:00 a.m.

"The prosecution calls Joseph Padrone," Crawford announced in his clear, crisp, confident voice as the forensic scientist stepped down.

Joe Padrone strode up to the witness box and was sworn in. His square shoulders and beefy frame created an impression of solidity. Nick knew that Padrone would impress the jury and his testimony would not be helpful to his case. Padrone was fiercely loyal to Samuel Wyndham, and Padrone was a man who never shifted loyalties. He felt protective toward Ruth as well.

Nick could have heard a pin drop in the courtroom as Padrone described the murder scene. Padrone had a lot of experience with death during his years in the NYPD as a narcotics detective. He knew that drugs led men to commit incredibly violent crimes. But despite his years as a cop, Padrone never reconciled himself to violence and murder. Such acts were a denial of everything civilized, everything Padrone believed in. He had joined the NYPD because he believed in just those principles of law and order that were perverted by every act of violence. Padrone was also experienced in loyalty. He had been involved in a drug bust with his partner, Ray Scasi, and the drugs had disappeared from police custody. They were never recovered. The press had a field day with the story. Someone had to go or it would look like the blue wall of silence again. Although there was no evidence to convict him, Padrone was pressured to take early retirement under a cloud of suspicion. Padrone was not guilty, but he knew who was. His partner was responsible. But Ray was dead, killed by an accomplice who left no trace and had never been identified.

Padrone had grown up with Ray on the streets of Brooklyn. He had been in love with Ray's girl. When she married Ray, Padrone made up his mind to remain a bachelor. And he did. Both Ray and his wife considered Padrone their closest friend and confidant. They asked him to be godfather to their son. Padrone would never blow the whistle on Ray and destroy his memory. It wouldn't change anything. And if he did, his widow and son would never live it down. Even worse, they would resent Padrone forever. To be sure, Padrone recognized that Ray was weak, that he had a gambling problem and needed money. But Padrone believed that Ray was a good person at heart and deep down never really thought of him as a criminal.

Padrone's loyalty to his partner cost him dearly. He came from a long line of New York City cops. When he was eleven years old, his father was killed in the line of duty. From that moment on he was determined to follow in his father's footsteps. To supplement her widow's pension, Padrone's mother found work as Samuel Wyndham's housekeeper and helped to raise Ruth after her mother's death. Gradually Wyndham took a personal interest in Padrone. He began to think of him as the son he never had. Padrone was intelligent, and when he graduated from high school, Wyndham offered to send him to college. But Padrone wanted to be a cop like his father. When Padrone retired from the department, Samuel Wyndham hired him to organize the Institute's security force. Wyndham had complete faith in Padrone and did not believe for a moment that he had been

"Aren't slide projectors out of date?"

"Yes, they are. And while the Institute, like all museums, has digitized its collection, film has better resolution and more accurate color than most digital images. If you are looking for subtle differences in photographed objects, film is preferable. A few companies still make high quality film," the former detective explained. "So the Institute continues to use film as well as digital imaging for studying objects, and especially for purposes of authentication."

"Please describe exactly where the defendant was standing and what he was doing," Crawford continued.

"He was directly behind Wyndham, in the doorway of the darkroom adjoining his office. The murder weapon was in his left hand."

Nick heard footsteps and the sound of the courtroom door closing. He turned and saw that Ruth was no longer there.

"Can you tell us about the murder weapon?" Crawford continued.

"Yes. It was one of two Minoan bronze axes in the collection. Peter Ryan, director of the Institute's laboratory, discovered one of the axes at the foot of a vandalized Egyptian statue."

"Vandalized statue?" Crawford paused for effect. "Can you tell us the nature of the vandalism?"

Padrone shifted uneasily, worried about the Institute's reputation as well as his own. "Well, it happened to a statue of the Buddha as well. In the Far Eastern Department."

"*What* happened, Mr. Padrone?" Crawford persisted.

"Both statues were decapitated." There was murmuring in the courtroom. The judge demanded silence.

Crawford was certain the jury would make the obvious connection between Wyndham's death and the decapitation of the statues. Nick was the obvious link.

Crawford decided to push Padrone as far as possible. "Now, Mr. Padrone, according to forensics, Samuel Wyndham was struck on the left side of the neck. Is that consistent with what you saw?"

"Yes, it is."

"And the blow would have been forceful?"

"Very."

"And could it have been delivered from behind by a left-handed person?"

"Objection!" Rogers was on his feet. "Prosecution is leading the witness."

"Sustained."

Nick felt the jurors' eyes on him. He knew their minds were already made up. The foreman nodded and made a note.

Crawford could not have hoped for a better witness. Despite Rogers's objections, the jurors were left with the distinct impression that Nick was guilty.

"No more questions, Your Honor." Crawford sat down.

"Does the defense wish to cross-examine the witness?"

"Yes, Your Honor," Rogers approached the stand.

"Was the vandalism you described, Mr. Padrone, reported to the police?"

"No."

"Can you tell us why not?"

"Samuel Wyndham preferred to avoid publicity. He wanted to protect the reputation of his Institute."

"And did he discover who the vandal was?"

"No, he did not. It could have been any one of the curators or their staff."

"Why is that?"

"Because they all had coded security keys and 24/7 access to the building. Samuel Wyndham insisted that he was an impeccable judge of character, and therefore anyone who worked for him must be entirely trustworthy, especially his curators."

"Were there any other unreported incidents?"

"Well, there was the forgery," Padrone replied.

"Forgery?" Rogers persisted.

"Yes, the mask from Mycenae. During the curators' meeting—"

"Mask from Mycenae?" Rogers interrupted. "Could you tell us what that is?"

"It was one of the most precious objects in the collection. Priceless, in fact. And made of pure gold. There is a similar one in the National Archaeological Museum in Athens. Most scholars believe it was made from the wax death mask of a king. But Mr. Wyndham discovered that a fake had been substituted. He called ..."

The noise in the courtroom drowned out Padrone.

The judge threatened to clear the court.

Padrone continued. "Mr. Wyndham called a meeting to discuss the vandalism and the mask. I warned him not to. In my opinion Mr. Wyndham was stirring up a hornet's nest."

"Objection!" Crawford leapt to his feet.

"Sustained." The judge glared at Padrone. "Mr. Padrone, you must limit yourself to the facts."

Rogers was pleased with Padrone's testimony. It had shown that there were other curators with possible motives to kill Wyndham.

"Your Honor, no more questions."

"Mr. Crawford, do you wish to redirect?"

"Yes, Your honor." Crawford did not like the new turn the trial was taking. He knew that he had to convince the jurors that Nick was the only curator with a real motive to kill Wyndham.

"To the best of your knowledge," Crawford began, "was anyone at the Institute the evening Samuel Wyndham was murdered? Besides yourself and Nicholas d'Abernon?"

"Well, that's hard to say. Anyone could have been there. Peter Ryan usually worked late in the lab," Padrone explained. "We searched the place after finding Mr. Wyndham, but it was empty. The only person who I know for sure was there was Ricardo Montoya. He's the pre-Colombian curator. He was working in his office across the hall from d'Abernon's."

"Mr. Padrone, please describe Mr. d'Abernon's office and tell us how many entrances it has."

"There is only one entrance leading to the corridor. Another door on the opposite wall leads into a darkroom. There's no other way into the darkroom."

"Would you tell the court, Mr. Padrone, what brought you to Nicholas d'Abernon's office that night?"

"Pure routine. I was making rounds, checking the hallways and offices. I heard clicking noises. D'Abernon's office is not usually occupied after hours. He doesn't stay late very often. And besides, I knew Mr. Wyndham was in danger, ever since the meeting with the curators when he announced that he was beginning an investigation into the vandalism and other problems at the Institute. I warned him not to bring them into the open. He wouldn't listen. And there was his argument with d'Abernon."

"Argument?" Crawford saw an opening. This was the kind of evidence he was looking for.

"Everyone knew about it. D'Abernon and Mr. Wyndham were heard arguing behind closed doors."

"Objection," Rogers interrupted. "Hearsay. The witness did not hear the argument."

"Sustained."

"No more questions."

The judge glanced at his watch. It was nearly 12:30 p.m. He adjourned the court for lunch until 2:00 p.m.

As Crawford gathered his papers, a messenger handed him a note. He was wanted on the phone. Crawford hurried from the courtroom, dodging reporters and photographers. The messenger led thim to a private office. The telephone receiver was off the hook. Crawford shut the door and picked up the receiver.

"Crawford here."

"No names, please. How's it going?" The deputy mayor did not have to identify himself.

"Fine. The defense hasn't got a thing. And Rogers is wet behind the ears. It's a piece of cake."

"Listen carefully. Your political future is on the line. Here's the position as of now. The trial has to be over before the exhibition opens. The mayor wants a conviction, and he wants it soon. He can't afford adverse publicity or loose ends. He can't afford to look as if he is soft on crime.

"Furthermore, as you know, he's attending the opening dinner and will be seated with the Israeli prime minister and the presidents of Egypt and China. The mayor's bid for the presidency of the United States is at stake. His platform is based on reducing national crime and international terrorism, and using institutions like the Wyndham Institute will showcase his interest in foreign cultures and, by implication, his expertise in foreign affairs."

"Look." Crawford was pacing back and forth. "I already know all this. Don't worry. The judge and jury are with us all the way."

"There's another thing."

"What?"

"A member of the cleaning staff at the Israeli consulate found a bomb in a cultural attaché's office. Fortunately it was dismantled before it went off, and we have kept the incident out of the papers. The Israelis don't know who planted the bomb."

"Yes, I see," said Crawford.

"No, you don't see. This is a case of sabotage from the outside. Someone wants trouble. Someone or some group of extremists want to prevent the kind of international cooperation that the mayor has made a key feature of his political platform."

"Got you." Crawford sat down. "No problems on this end."

CHAPTER 6

Thursday, November 18, 1:00 p.m.

Ruth sat outside the courtroom. The doors opened as the crowd filed out for the lunch recess. She was besieged by a mob of reporters and press photographers. She made good copy. Not only was she the daughter of Samuel P. Wyndham, but she was one of the up-and-coming young fashion designers putting New York on a par with Paris and Milan as a couture capital of the world. She had that rare combination of talent, beauty, and connections that appealed to the public's insatiable appetite for reading about the rich and famous. When such people are beset by tragedy, the public becomes even hungrier, and journalists are only too happy to provide the necessary nourishment.

"Ruth." A hand tapped her shoulder.

She turned from the circle of newsmen and encountered Ricardo Montoya, curator of pre-Colombian art at the Institute. She was grateful for the interruption, and the look of friendly sympathy on Ricardo's face reassured her. She thought he was remarkably handsome, in a dark, Latin way. She could see why he was billed as one of New York's most eligible bachelors.

"Will you join me for dinner tonight?" he asked.

"Oh no, Ricardo. Thank you. I couldn't. I would be terrible company."

"But you have to eat." Ricardo was never pushy, though he could be persuasive. He was polite, gracious, and suave.

Ruth shook her head.

"How about a drink then?"

Ruth was too distracted to answer. She found it impossible to think about anything in the noisy hallway. A reporter thrust a microphone in front of her and demanded a statement. Ricardo put his arm around Ruth's shoulders and escorted her past the reporters.

A court officer approached Ruth. "Miss Wyndham," he said, "may I speak with you?"

"Yes, of course." Ruth stepped aside, putting space between herself and the crowd. The officer's appearance was a welcome excuse not to have to deal with the reporters—or Ricardo.

"Mr. d'Abernon's lawyer has requested a meeting between you and his client."

Ruth nodded.

"This way," he instructed with reassuring authority.

Ruth followed him through a maze of corridors. She had only one thought: how to prove Nick's innocence. She went over and over the events of her father's murder. It had to have been someone at the Institute, but who? Her father had trusted all of them.

A heavy door banged shut and the loud noise jolted Ruth back to the moment at hand. She followed the officer into a bare room, where Nick was seated at a metal table.

"Thank you for coming," Rogers said. "I'll leave you two alone for a few minutes." He turned to the officer standing guard in the corner. "It's all right," Rogers said. "You can wait just outside."

Ruth sat down opposite Nick.

"I'm sorry about the things you heard in court this morning," Nick began.

"It's okay. I left after a while. I couldn't listen anymore. I had to get some air."

Ruth was struck by how different Nick appeared in the cold, drab room. Paint was peeling from the olive-green walls. The windows were barred and a dull gray light filtered through the grimy panes. A single light bulb hung from the ceiling. Usually confident and athletic, Nick now looked thin, even shrunken, as he hunched over, his head heavy on his shoulders. It was so unlike the self-assured scholar who, until his arrest, had been assistant director of the Wyndham Institute.

Ruth went straight to the point. "Listen, Nick, I want to know what you argued about with my father after the curators' meeting."

"I can't tell you. I can't tell anyone. Besides, it had nothing to do with his murder."

"Nick, it's important. It could save your life. What about us? What about our future together? Do you want to spend the rest of your life in jail? Where does that leave me? Where does it leave us?"

"Ruth, that's not fair! I tell you everything. This one time I can't. Please believe me. You know I care about us. And we will find a way out of this mess. I promise."

"If you won't tell me, then at least let me hire a more experienced lawyer to defend you. Chris Rogers is trying his best, but he's not in the same league as Crawford."

"We've been through this before, Ruth, and you know my answer."

"Why must you be so stubborn? It's not just your life that's at stake here." Ruth shook her head in frustration. "Once you make up your mind, nothing changes it. You're just like father that way."

Nick took her hand in his. Ruth let it linger in his grasp. It felt comfortable, as if they fit together. The guard knocked on the door and opened it to signal the end of the meeting. Ruth rose, kissed Nick, and left quickly.

The faint scent of her Calèche perfume lingered in the air. Nick slumped back in his chair. He had struggled his whole life to succeed, to make something of himself, and this was where he ended up. For as long as he could remember, money had been a problem. And now it was an even bigger problem with lawyers' fees and the expense of the trial. He had hired the best lawyer he could afford. If my father had lived, Nick thought, things would have been different.

"Might have beens are useless," Nick told himself. "And so is self-pity." He thought about his mother. At least her death had spared her the ordeal of the trial. He was thankful for that. She had lived through enough. Her Jewish parents had survived World War II, hidden from the Nazis by local farmers in Czechoslovakia. She was born after the war and raised in Prague. Her parents encouraged her to escape to the West when the Soviets crushed the 1968 uprising.

Nick smiled in spite of himself as he remembered his mother's description of her unlikely meeting with his father. It happened on a cold, overcast day in February 1972. She had not been in New York long before she met Robert d'Abernon, scion of a wealthy family from Richmond, Virginia. Robert was on a three-day pass from McGuire Air Force Base. Like all the men in his family, he was a graduate of the Citadel and headed for a military career.

As Robert strolled along a narrow street in Greenwich Village, he came upon a curious sight. Through the window of a Laundromat he saw a strikingly beautiful, dark-haired young woman fighting with a washing machine. She banged her fists on the controls and kicked the door. The machine fought back. Robert was riveted. He watched as a puff of soapsuds bubbled up and began to seep out through the door. In a matter of seconds the soapsuds covered the floor up to the girl's ankles. She took off her shoes and stared down at the suds as Robert entered.

"Robert d'Abernon, at your service." He bowed in the manner of a Southern cavalier.

The girl was too furious to speak coherently. Robert couldn't hide his amusement. He was charmed by the dark-haired girl, whose foreign accent was just noticeable enough to be intriguing. She, despite her frustration, had to admit that the man before her was handsome, tall and dark with deep-blue eyes. She forgot about the soapsuds. "Naomi Mendelssohn at yours," she replied with a smile.

That was the beginning of a whirlwind romance that led to the marriage bureau. The newlyweds were not destined to spend much time together, only a few short weeks while Robert flew training missions. Then they were transferred to a military base in Colorado.

Robert's parents did not share his enthusiasm for Naomi. In fact, they were appalled. They refused to meet her. D'Abernon men did not marry Northerners or foreigners and especially not Jewish foreigners. By the time Robert died in a training accident, he had been disinherited by his parents. They were convinced that Naomi was a fortune hunter. She was five months pregnant at the time of the accident. Her son resembled his father—the same dark hair and deep blue eyes—and she named him Nicholas.

Naomi moved to Denver and found work as a piano teacher. Her widow's benefits from the military helped her survive and educate Nick. He was a brilliant student who went through school on scholarships. After college, Nick studied the archaeology of the Ancient Near East and Minoan Crete at Stanford. His academic performance soon attracted the attention of his professors, and it was not long before he was spending every summer working on archaeological excavations. Eventually he directed his own dig on Crete and published his findings in what became a standard monograph on the cross-cultural ties between the ancient Near Eastern and Minoan civilizations.

When Nick was invited to present his conclusions at the 2004 International Archaeological Congress in Rome, he met Samuel Wyndham. Wyndham was impressed by his young colleague and proposed dinner. The reputation of the Wyndham Institute was well known to Nick, as it was to scholars throughout the world. An invitation from Samuel Wyndham was not to be taken lightly.

"The Wyndham Institute needs an assistant director," Wyndham had said with his typical decisiveness. "And you seem to have the qualifications I'm looking for."

Of all the possible career paths that Nick had considered, the Wyndham Institute was by far the most prestigious. Samuel Wyndham was the most remarkable and accomplished scholar in a field he had virtually created: the combination of paleoanthropology, the study of early man with archaeology, the study of early civilizations, and the cultural sciences, which could be integrated into the other two studies. Such combinations and interdisciplinary approaches, in Samuel's view, would lead to new avenues of research and yield new information on the nature of humanity. His work had led to the discovery that made him famous.

Then Nick met Ruth.

CHAPTER 7

June 16, 2004

Ruth had accompanied her father to the Archaeological Congress in Rome. Nick was attracted to her at once. She was dark and vibrant. Her short, black hair framed her face like a cameo. She had large, brown, laughing eyes, which set off her delicate skin. Her tall, graceful figure was that of an athlete. Nick understood Samuel Wyndham's pride when he introduced Ruth. They spoke briefly, and then Samuel whisked his daughter off to attend a paper on improved techniques in dendrochronology, the science of dating cultures according to tree rings, and the uranium-thorium method of dating.

Both dendrochronology and the uranium-thorium method were discovered after Carbon 14, which can only be used to date organic material containing the radioactive isotope of carbon. By analyzing the amount of Carbon 14 present in organic matter, it is possible to extrapolate backward to the time an object was produced. In the case of fossils or bone fragments, Carbon 14 can be an accurate technique. But Carbon 14 cannot be used for nonorganic substances such as marble, bronze, and gold. For those materials, dendrochronology or the uranium-thorium method are preferable. Dating objects according to the number of tree rings on the tree fossils discovered at sites makes it possible to estimate the age of nonorganic material. Where no tree fossils exist, the uranium-thorium method allows scientists to date objects by analyzing the calcium carbonate or calcite found in adjacent rocks or on cave surfaces. But no matter how accurate the technology, once a nonorganic artifact is removed from its original site, there is no foolproof method for dating it. As a result, Nick knew, it was more difficult to prove that objects made of stone and metals were forgeries.

Nick regretted having promised to attend a meeting on Minoan bronzes chaired by one of his friends from Stanford. He would have much preferred to accompany the Wyndhams.

Later that same evening Nick saw Ruth again at the reception at the American Academy organized by the mayor of Rome. Ruth was at the edge of the dance floor, drinking champagne and chatting animatedly with an Italian archaeologist.

Nick could not take his eyes off Ruth's dress. It was plum-colored, soft and filmy, and embroidered with delicate gold and silver herons. It molded itself to her every curve. Nick reintroduced himself and asked her to dance.

"That's a lovely dress," he said, whisking her away from the archaeologist.

Ruth laughed. "It's my own design. I used the Institute's collection of Japanese kimonos for inspiration."

The orchestra struck up a waltz. Nick followed the music and swept Ruth up in its rhythms. He was delighted with her ability to follow his every turn. As they spun around the floor, Nick saw his own exhilaration reflected in Ruth's expression. For a moment no one existed except the two of them whirling around the Baroque ballroom under crystal chandeliers. The music stopped, but it was a few seconds before they realized it. When they did, they found themselves at the center of the dance floor with the other guests smiling and clapping in a circle around them.

After the reception, Nick took Ruth for a walk along the banks of the Tiber. It was a soft, warm night, its calm broken only by the occasional revving of a motorcycle. The imposing Castel Sant'Angelo, the mausoleum of the emperor Hadrian, loomed up from across the river. It was eerily illuminated by lights from the bridge. Nick found himself telling Ruth about his boyhood in Aspen, about the mountains covered with wild flowers in spring and blanketed with snow in winter. He described the small, sleepy town it had been before being discovered by ski enthusiasts and falling prey to real-estate developers.

Nick paused, sensing that his childhood was dull in comparison to Ruth's. Hers had been saturated with wealth, social position, and success. Nick still resented the way his father's parents had treated his mother and the fact that they had completely ignored him. He tried to persuade himself that he wanted as little to do with them as they did with him. Yet, their indifference to his existence was a source of sadness and disappointment. But Ruth was no snob, and when Nick asked about her past, she made him realize that in some ways he had been the fortunate one.

"My father is a rich man," she said simply. "I grew up in a townhouse on East Seventy-Eighth Street in Manhattan and attended an elite private school. But I felt a bit like Rapunzel, isolated in a tower. People seemed to think I led a glamorous life. But it wasn't so wonderful. I had very few friends. My classmates were jealous of me, and I didn't help. I was shy and must have seemed like a snob myself."

Ruth paused, surprised that a stroll along the Tiber with a man she hardly knew should so vividly arouse her childhood memories. She looked up at Nick. "You know," she said, "I think I might envy the way you grew up. You never had to question your mother's love. My mother died in a car accident when I was three."

"But your father is devoted to you. Anyone can see that."

"Yes. I know that now. But it was different when I was a child. I felt there was a barrier between us. He never seemed at ease with me. I used to catch him staring at me when he thought I didn't notice. And I imagined that he was comparing me to her. My mother was beautiful. I used to sneak into my father's bedroom when he was away and study her pictures. He kept them on his bureau in silver Tiffany frames. I wanted to look just like her. She was blonde with blue eyes and a radiant smile. Whenever I saw those pictures, I was acutely aware of how unlike her and awkward I was."

"That was a long time ago," Nick said. "You certainly aren't the child you were now. I suppose your father was busy with the Institute. He has accomplished a great deal."

"That is certainly true. There were endless meetings and conferences, international lecture tours, and excavations in the summer. Sometimes I didn't see him for months at a time. I actually hated the Institute when I was younger. I couldn't understand why my father seemed more interested in it than me. Selfish, I guess, but what child isn't?"

"Didn't you have any friends?"

"In the tenth grade, right in the middle of the fall term, my father sent me to boarding school. He thought he was doing me a favor. He said I needed to be with other girls and not spend so much time alone when he was away. And our housekeeper, Joe's mother, was ready to retire. I was convinced my father was trying to get rid of me when what I most needed was his company. His life was so crowded with important matters that he seemed to have no time for an awkward adolescent."

"And when did the awkward adolescent turn into the lovely Ruth Wyndham?"

"This must be boring you to death, Nick. Let's change the subject. Aren't you tired of hearing about me?"

"Not at all. I told you my life story, now it's your turn."

"All right. But don't say I didn't warn you. It gets worse before it gets better."

"Press on, MacRuth."

"Well, boarding school was a disaster. I was alone all the time. Life at home began to seem like paradise. Arriving in the middle of a term was a terrible idea. All the girls had picked their friends and divided up into cliques. I would have much preferred a coed school. The only boy I knew was Joe, Joe Padrone, and I missed his company enormously."

Nick looked vaguely annoyed.

"Joe was our housekeeper's son. I thought he was perfect."

"Thought or think?" asked Nick. He sounded worried.

Ruth smiled. "Joe was like a big brother in a fairy tale." She hoped Nick was satisfied, and maybe just a little jealous. "Joe gave me piggyback rides and took me sledding in the park. In spring we rode the carousel and he bought me helium balloons and Cracker Jacks. We always argued over the prize at the bottom of the box. Joe was good at homework too. He helped me every night. When I went to boarding school, he was the only one who wrote regularly."

"He certainly sounds attentive." Nick was clearly concerned.

"All the other girls had boyfriends who wrote to them. They came up on prom weekends and took them out on dates. I didn't have any dates in boarding school and never went to a prom. The day I graduated from Essex Academy—that was the name of the school—was the best day of my life. Father managed to come to graduation, so did Joe and his mother, and they helped me pack. When our chauffeur pulled out of the driveway, I didn't look back or have a single regret.

"But you know, Nick, it's funny. After all that, I did learn something really important at boarding school. I found, to my surprise, that I enjoy my own company."

"I rather like it myself," Nick said.

"I also discovered that I love to draw. At graduation, my father asked what had become of the 'ugly duckling.' He was still joking about my appearance. But, for the first time, I had the feeling that he was proud of me. It felt wonderful.

"And he encouraged my interest in fashion. The following fall I went to Parson's School of Design."

"So," Nick said. "That's when you decided to rifle museums for fashion ideas?"

"It seemed a logical thing to do. The old patterns are too beautiful to remain embalmed in museum cases. They are just asking to be let out and given new life."

"I suppose you spent all your time studying?" Nick said hopefully.

"Oh, I don't know," Ruth said casually. "I had the usual round of dates ..." Her voice trailed off as her mind drifted to the early days at Parson's.

"I get the feeling you're a million miles away." Nick jolted Ruth back to Rome. They were just then passing by Trajan's Forum on their way to the pensione.

"I'm sorry, Nick. I got lost in the past for a moment."

"It must have been quite a past."

"No, really, it was nothing." Ruth decided not to tell Nick about the unhappy romance of her student days.

"This is a pretty nice moment right now," she said as Nick guided her to the foot of the monumental column proclaiming Trajan's victories over his enemies. "By the way, Nick, did you know that the Wyndham Institute owns two of the gold helmets that Trajan looted from the Dacians, those skilled metalworkers living in what is now Romania?"

"And, Ruth, did you know that Trajan used what he stole from the Dacians to set up a retirement colony in Algeria for his soldiers?"

"No. I had no idea that retirement communities existed that far back, but if you look closely you can see some of those lucky soldiers taking prisoners." Ruth pointed to a section of the marble relief.

They continued through the forum, one of the few couples still there.

Ruth had been thinking a lot about Nick since meeting him that morning. His attentiveness at the reception, the waltz, and the stroll along the Tiber all charmed her. As she listened to the account of Nick's childhood in Aspen, she sensed his energy and curiosity. She was flattered by his concentration on what she said and by the way he stooped slightly as he listened.

"How about a night cap?" Nick suggested. "My pensione is not far from here."

Ruth was booked into the conference hotel where her father was also staying. But she was happy to prolong the evening with Nick.

"I'd love one," she replied.

When they arrived at his pensione, Nick punched in the security code, and the heavy wooden doors swung open onto a cobblestone courtyard. They entered the spacious lobby that had once been a grand dining hall.

"Wait right here," Nick said. "I'll get some drinks."

Ruth settled into an old brocade sofa in the corner.

Though it had seen better days, the room retained traces of its former magnificence. The high ceiling was decorated with a large, painted medallion depicting Mars kneeling at the feet of a reclining Venus. At the four corners of the ceiling, Cupid assumed four different poses as he drew back his bow and aimed an arrow directly at the war god's torso. The walls were divided into panels framed by intricately carved, gilded stucco designs. Each panel contained allegories of mythological figures. But the unmistakable evidence of rising damp and peeling paint depressed Ruth. The owner clearly could not afford to keep the building in good repair.

Nick returned with two long-stemmed wine glasses and a bottle of Prosecco. He sat down beside Ruth and filled the glasses with the sparkling wine. "Here's to Rome and to aging pensiones." Nick leaned over and kissed Ruth on the forehead. She pulled back, gazed into his intense blue eyes, and then felt his lips gently press against hers.

Ruth did not sleep at her hotel that night. She woke up early the next morning wrapped in Nick's arms. At first she was confused, and then it all came back. The side of her face was pressed tightly against Nick's chest and she could hear his regular breathing and feel his lungs expand and contract. She lay completely still, remembering the night before and the tenderness and joy that had flooded over her. She was caught up in the memory when she felt Nick move. He began stroking her back and hair. He kissed her softly.

Ruth buried herself deeper in Nick's arms. She was too happy and too lazy to speak. She kissed his chest and moved her hand lightly up and down his thigh. It seemed as if the night had never ended.

CHAPTER 8

"Look, Chris, I know Tariq is up to something." Nick and his lawyer sat in the room reserved for prisoners while the court was adjourned.

"That's all very well, Nick, but where's your proof? What exactly do you have in mind? We have ten minutes until court reconvenes." Chris Rogers glanced apprehensively at his Timex. "What do you want me to do?"

"I really don't know." Nick slumped in his chair. "I've told you everything I know. And with the case coming to trial so fast, we didn't have much chance to prepare. Though I must admit, I don't even know where to begin trying to prove my innocence."

"Never mind about that now. Tell me what you know about Tariq." Nadim Tariq was the tall, slim, dark-haired curator of ancient Egyptian archaeology at the Institute. Nick admired his extensive knowledge of the field, but he had always found him short-tempered and uncommunicative.

"Well, you remember I told you that after the curators' meeting Tariq asked me to sign for a package being delivered that afternoon? He said he had to be away from the Institute. When the package came, I opened it to make sure it was the object I signed for. At first I thought it was a joke. Why else would a hieroglyphic inscription be inserted in the middle of a completely banal lab report and provenance for an ordinary Coptic glass bowl? The Copts didn't write hieroglyphics; they were, and still are, Christians. They didn't even know how to read hieroglyphics. The key had been lost centuries before the Copts appeared in Egypt and were not understood again until Napoleon's army discovered the Rosetta Stone. And why had the Alexandria Museum sent Tariq the bowl in the first place? There are several similar but far more valuable bowls in the Institute's collection already. We certainly didn't need another one.

"I don't know all that much about hieroglyphics, but something about the way that particular inscription was written was all wrong. The symbols weren't in the order one usually expects, and the normal connecting signs were missing. It seemed more like a code. The whole thing made me suspicious enough to wait for Tariq's return and follow him when he left the Institute. I'm no sleuth and maybe my imagination was running away with me, but so much was going on at the time that I began to wonder if Tariq might be the one stealing and forging objects. I didn't even think about the vandalism.

"Anyway, I followed him to a local Middle Eastern restaurant. He was carrying the package, and when he arrived, he struck up a conversation with two men sitting at the bar. I saw him pass it to one of them. When I returned to the Institute, damned if the bowl wasn't on Tariq's desk! But the provenance and the inscription were gone. I can't even be sure it was the same bowl, because as I said, there are several similar ones in the Institute's collections, and not everything has been catalogued yet. That was one of Tariq's jobs."

"We have to go to court now, Nick. I'll see what I can do."

Sinclair Crawford sat down. He was immensely satisfied with his examination of Nadim Tariq. Although Tariq had not overheard the argument between Nick and Wyndham, he had managed to put Nick in a bad light by insinuating that Nick would do anything to become director of the Wyndham Institute. This was exactly what Crawford had hoped for.

"Mr. Tariq," Chris Rogers began his cross-examination slowly. "I want you to remember that you are still under oath."

Nadim Tariq squared his shoulders, sat bolt upright, and bristled at the implied insult.

Nick saw Nadim's dark eyes narrow. He knew only too well how sensitive Nadim Tariq was to any suspected slur on his character and integrity. And he realized that Nadim could be extremely dangerous when cornered. Nadim's testimony confirmed Nick's impression that he would do anything to see Nick convicted, including committing perjury.

"Mr. Tariq." Rogers proceeded, seemingly oblivious to the resentment he had inspired. "Have you ever taken objects from the Institute's collections out of the Institute?"

"I most certainly have not!" Nadim Tariq protested. Nick saw his knuckles whiten as he gripped the arms of the witness chair.

"Mr. Tariq," continued Rogers calmly, "is it not true that on the evening of September 1, indeed the very date of the curators' meeting, you went to the Oasis Restaurant on Second Avenue and Sixty-Fourth Street?"

So he had been right! D'Abernon *had* been following him. Nadim was too well trained to panic. He knew he had to stay calm. Whatever Nick had seen or suspected, there was no way that he could really know what was going on.

"Mr. Rogers, I often go to the Oasis. I like the food. It reminds me of home."

"I asked whether you were there on the evening of September 1. You have not answered my question. Perhaps I can refresh your memory by reminding you that on that evening you met two gentlemen at the bar. You ordered a Diet Coke, and as you were waiting for it, you handed a package—a package that you had brought with you from the Wyndham Institute—to one of them. He then left the restaurant and took the package with him."

"Are you accusing me of stealing the Institute's property?" demanded the outraged Nadim. "Is it a crime in a free country to give presents to one's friends?"

"Mr. Tariq." Rogers paused. "I am referring to the issue of theft from the Institute."

"Objection!" roared Sinclair Crawford over the titters of the spectators. "Mr. Rogers is making a most improper insinuation and implying a conclusion for which he has absolutely no proof."

"Sustained," thundered the judge. "Mr. Rogers, you will find yourself facing disciplinary action if you continue on this course."

"I apologize, Your Honor. No more questions."

Rogers returned to the defense table. He wished he could have done more to discredit Nadim Tariq. All he had to go on was what Nick saw at the Oasis, which did not amount to much. That was the problem with the entire case. Sure, there were a lot of nasty things going on at the Wyndham Institute, but where was the proof? Where was the evidence that someone besides Nick had a clear-cut motive to murder Samuel Wyndham? Rogers did not know what more he could do for his client.

Nadim Tariq seethed with rage as he stormed off the witness stand. He mustered every ounce of self-control to suppress his fury. He was ready to kill Chris Rogers, and he hoped that Nick d'Abernon would rot in hell. How dare that bastard lawyer suggest that he, Nadim Tariq, was smuggling goods out of the Institute, and how dare he imply that Nadim was operating at the level of an ordinary thief? Nadim knew that he had been absolutely right to have been wary of d'Abernon. It was stupid to have asked him for a favor. Nick had been on to something all along. But, Nadim wondered, how much did Nick really know?

Nadim's mind raced. Now that he had testified, he was free to leave. He had to reach his contact fast, explain the situation, and decide how to proceed. The publicity of the trial was a big problem, but there was still time to capitalize on the information that had arrived that morning from Cairo. That is, as long as he could be sure d'Abernon did not know more than he let on. At least he was stuck in a jail cell, a fact that gave Nadim great satisfaction.

Nadim paused a moment as the courtroom doors closed behind him. He reached into his jacket pocket and pulled out his cell phone. His footsteps echoed on the marble floor as he hurried down the corridor.

CHAPTER 9

Thursday, November 18, 4:00 p.m.

Nick watched Peter Ryan, the Institute's chemist and laboratory technician, amble up to the witness box. He had to smile. Nothing can make that man hurry, Nick thought, especially not the law. Peter was a law unto himself. He did not give a damn about conventions of any sort. If he had, he would never dress as he did. Peter Ryan had been wearing L.L. Bean clothes for years, long before they became fashionable. But they never quite fit. His brown corduroy trousers were belted just above his hips and hung down over the heels of his scuffed brown boots. His black spandex turtleneck did nothing to disguise an incipient beer belly. Peter was not fat, but he did drink a lot of beer, and it was settling into an expanding paunch.

Peter wiped his forehead with his back-pocket handkerchief. The man certainly did sweat. Too damn much beer! And the occasional joint didn't help. Nick thought of all the times he had visited Peter in the lab. As they discussed the chemical procedures for testing artifacts, Peter would produce an endless array of beer from the fridge. Sometimes Ruth joined them. If Nick were not in his office, she could be pretty sure he was in Peter's lab, indulging in an Anchor Steam beer or an Amstel. Peter knew his beer as well as he knew his chemicals. He had even written out Blake's couplet and pasted in onto the door of the fridge: "Malt does more than Milton can/to justify God's ways to man."

Peter was the closest thing the Wyndham Institute had to a court jester. He was gregarious, just a little coarse, and always ready with a joke. Peter got along with everyone at the Institute, which made it all the more surprising, Nick thought, that there was a strain between him and Nadim. Probably Nadim's puritanical nature, Nick told himself. Nadim thoroughly disapproved of all drugs and alcohol. He was also impeccably neat and probably found Peter's casual style irritating.

Peter was a wonderful mimic; his imitation of Samuel Wyndham in one of his more dictatorial moods was particularly good. He got what he called the "Boston Backbone" to a tee. He also did a good takeoff on Ricardo Montoya, "the Colombian Romeo," as Peter referred to him. After a few beers and a bit of encouragement, Peter would launch into his soft-shoe routine, a smooth shuffle across the laboratory floor, ending with a slow-motion pirouette.

Peter was older than Nick by a good ten years, but somehow Nick always thought of him as younger. He had the round, innocent face of a baby. His blue eyes and light-brown, unruly hair added to his youthful appearance. Nick had not been able to resist joking about Peter's baby face when he noticed an entire shelf of pure cornstarch baby powder and aloe hand cream in one of the cupboards.

"I guess that explains your peaches and cream complexion," Nick had said.

"With my odd hours and all the stuff I've got to test, I spend a lot of time here. In fact, that couch you're sitting on pulls out into a bed. A man's got to shower and shave in the morning. I need a complete supply of beauty equipment."

"A whole shelf of baby powder? And aloe?"

"If it's good enough for babies, it's good enough for me. Non-allergenic. Besides," Peter added with a grin, "nursing babies are just about the only members of the human race that the great American consumer society is not supposed to poison with drugs and additives, although it does happen. The aloe helps with the chemicals I get on my hands testing objects for forgeries."

Nick had always been puzzled by the combination of Peter's brilliance and lack of ambition. It was one thing to be a curator at the Wyndham Institute, but for a chemist the job was routine. Perhaps it had been the first Gulf War. Sometimes Nick found himself thinking that Peter's stint in the army and his time in Iraq had drained his ambition and accounted for his cynical attitude toward just about everything. Peter was cynical about politics, money, work, and women. Or perhaps there was something in Peter's past. When Nick thought about it, for all their conversations and the time they spent together, he knew very little about Peter.

Peter finally made it to the witness box. He refused to take an oath on the Bible, which he referred to as the "war-games manual." The judge was not amused.

Sinclair Crawford went to work. His words rang in Nick's ears. The courtroom seemed so far from reality that Nick wondered if he were losing his grip.

Nick suddenly realized that Peter was staring at him. He snapped out of his reverie in time to hear Crawford ask Peter if he was a willing witness.

"No," Peter replied. "I am not a willing witness. I don't believe for a moment that Nick d'Abernon had anything to do with Samuel Wyndham's death."

Good old Peter, thought Nick.

"Mr. Ryan, we are not interested in what you think, only in

facts. I would be grateful if you would confine yourself to answering the questions."

Peter gave Crawford a look of palpable disgust.

"Mr. Ryan, is it true that you overheard the argument between Samuel Wyndham and Nicholas d'Abernon?"

Peter paused. He knew how damaging his testimony would be for Nick. He liked Nick as much as he liked anyone, but he would not put himself on the line for him or anybody else. And neither, as far as he knew, would anyone else at the Wyndham Institute. The curators had every reason to want Wyndham dead and Nick convicted. And so did he. It will be interesting, thought Peter, to see poor old Nick's ass nailed to the wall. He should have learned by now that tilting at windmills is a fool's game.

"Back off, Nick old boy," Peter would say whenever Nick complained about the ethics of the museum world. "Stop playing God. This is the real world, and it stinks. There's no such thing as honor these days."

"Look, Peter, I know what you're trying to say. But the reputation of the Institute is at stake."

And where did your high-minded principles get you? thought Peter. Look where you are now. And where does that leave Ruth? With Wyndham dead and Nick out of the way, Peter began to believe that he just might have a chance with her. But as long as Nick was around, Ruth would be beyond his grasp.

Peter knew that no one could be trusted. Loyalty meant nothing when it came to money. He never forgot his father's descent into alcoholism and his eventual suicide. Shortly after World War II, his father had developed a patent for a hydrogen-based alternate fuel that would help to eliminate America's dependence on foreign oil. He sank all of his money into research. But because his resources were limited, he joined forces with a firm of venture capitalists. Only later did Peter's father find out that his inability to obtain a patent on the process was due to the direct intervention of one of the partners, who was a large stockholder in American and Middle Eastern oil companies. The partner's election to the US Senate the following year hinged on the financial support of the oil industry and its government lobbyists.

"Mr. Ryan, will you please address yourself to the question?"

Pompous ass, thought Peter. He gazed at Nick and shrugged.

"Yes, I did hear them arguing. The old man had a terrific temper."

"Mr. Ryan, just answer the question, please! Do not editorialize. Tell us exactly what you heard."

"Well, the old man was threatening Nick. I only caught a few words."

"What few words did you hear?" Sinclair Crawford persisted. He did not like Peter Ryan any more than Peter Ryan liked him. But Crawford had the advantage. Peter reminded him of a fish wriggling on the end of a hook; Crawford coaxed him gently into his net. It was child's play.

"Well," Peter said as he stared at the window, "all I heard was the old man saying 'If you persist in what you are doing, I will not hesitate to rescind your appointment. I'll throw you out of this Institute and see to it that you never get another job.'"

A choice few words, thought Nick, glancing at the jurors. All twelve jurors were riveted. Nick knew how damaging the testimony about the argument was. He was the one person who could explain it, but he would not.

"Thank you, Mr. Ryan. There is no need to detain you any longer." Sinclair Crawford returned to his seat with an expression of deep satisfaction on his chiseled face.

Nick's attorney rose slowly to his feet and approached Peter.

"Mr. Ryan, would you please tell us your position at the Wyndham Institute and describe to the jury what you do?"

"Certainly," Peter's manner changed. He relaxed and slouched in his seat. He was his old, genial self. Now he seemed eager to talk.

"I'm in charge of the laboratory. I perform chemical tests on the objects that come into the Institute to confirm their authenticity."

"Thank you, Mr. Ryan. Were you present at the meeting of curators convened by Mr. Wyndham shortly before his death?"

"Yes, I was," said Peter.

"Were you aware beforehand of the reason for the meeting?"

"Yes. Samuel had come to see me two weeks earlier with several objects he believed had been tampered with. One was a Chinese Bronze Age cauldron from the thirteenth century BC. The cauldron was real enough in terms of its date and the stylized dragon patterns on the surface. But it didn't match the description provided by its previous owner."

"Could you explain to the court exactly what you mean?"

"Certainly. The description identified the origin of the cauldron as the Anyang site northwest of Shanghai. Anyang was the last capital of the Shang Dynasty. But the patina on the bronze indicated that it must have been buried in soil from a very different part of China. When Wyndham pursued the matter, he found that there was no excavation record of this particular cauldron."

Rogers paused to let the information sink in, and then said, "Are you suggesting, Mr. Ryan, that someone at the Institute has been involved in vandalizing archaeological sites and smuggling objects into the United States?"

Sinclair Crawford jumped to his feet. "Objection, Your Honor! This line of questioning is irrelevant. The charge in this trial is murder, not smuggling."

"On the contrary, Your Honor," retorted Rogers. "I contend that this line of questioning is entirely relevant. I will show that there were a number of irregularities occurring at the Institute, and that these had come to the attention of Samuel Wyndham shortly before he called the meeting. It is my contention that in pursuing these so-called 'irregularities' we shall see that there were others with stronger motives for murder than those ascribed to Mr. d'Abernon."

Murmurs filled the courtroom as the implications of Rogers's allegation sank in.

Well, well, thought Nick, good old Chris. He's learning from Crawford. He certainly let the cat among the pigeons. The only problem is, where do we go from here? Suspicion and innuendo are all very well, but we need facts. And fact number one is that Joe Padrone discovered me at the murder scene with the ax in my hand.

"Silence in the courtroom!" The judge banged his gavel. He turned to Crawford. "Objection overruled."

"Thank you, Your Honor." Rogers smiled. He addressed Peter again. "Mr. Ryan, did Samuel Wyndham show you any other objects he had reason to doubt?"

"Yes, he did. Wyndham brought me two faïence statuettes of a figure of the Minoan Snake Goddess with gold snakes entwined around her arms. We discovered that both statuettes were ancient, but the snakes were not. Instead of the original gold snakes, forgeries of pyrite had been substituted."

"Pyrite?"

"It's known as fool's gold."

Once again the spectators stirred and whispered. And once again the judge called for order.

Nick saw that Peter was enjoying every minute on the stand, and especially the sensation caused by his testimony. He would, Nick thought. It's the performer in him.

"You may proceed, Mr. Ryan," instructed the judge.

"The discovery that the snakes were forgeries led Wyndham to examine the gold Mycenaean mask. We discovered that that was also forged—that it was pyrite and not gold. But I must say it was done by a very skilled forger. Then Wyndham asked me to test all the ancient jewelry and any other gold objects for contamination or outright forgery."

Rogers paced back and forth to give Peter's testimony time to register.

Perhaps there is hope for you, thought Nick. With effort and practice, maybe good old Chris Rogers would acquire some of Crawford's confidence and dramatic flair.

"So, Mr. Ryan, would you say that Samuel Wyndham had reason to believe there was something seriously wrong at the Institute?"

"Definitely."

"Did you believe that Mr. Wyndham had reason to fear for his safety?"

"Samuel did not take me into his confidence, although he did ask me not to discuss our conversations with anyone. But it seems to me that, yes, there were plenty of people at the Institute that Wyndham should have been worried about."

"Objection!" shouted Sinclair Crawford.

"Sustained."

"Thank you, Mr. Ryan. No more questions."

It was 6:00 p.m. The judge was due at Gracie Mansion for dinner at 6:30 p.m. He adjourned the court until Friday at 10:00 a.m.

CHAPTER 10

Thursday, November 18, 6:00 p.m.

N adim Tariq tapped his foot impatiently as he waited on line in the crowded cafeteria. The steam from the food displays hung in the air like a dank cloud and condensed into wet patches on the plate glass window blocking the view of the snow-covered street. The Bellmont Cafeteria had been one of the first places Nadim discovered in downtown Manhattan. The food was cheap and tolerable. Such a motley assortment of people ate there that nothing and no one would look suspicious. Derelicts, drunks, drug addicts of all ages and stages sat huddled at the Formica tables, nursing cups of coffee, killing time, and waiting to be readmitted to the shelter down the block. Students from New York University congregated in groups, talking and arguing. A number of regulars—taxi drivers, midlevel businessmen, and bearded academics in rumpled turtlenecks—ate with a newspaper or book propped up in front of them.

Nadim spotted his contact sitting alone at a table in the rear. The short, pudgy man repulsed Nadim, who found it hard to conceal his disgust. Nadim observed beads of perspiration glistening on top of the man's greasy, bald forehead as he speared the apple pie à la mode he invariably ordered. It was a dish he had first eaten in America and for which he had developed a passion.

Nadim paid for his yogurt and coffee and edged his way around the tables with his tray. He slipped into the empty chair opposite his contact. For a while neither man spoke. Nadim watched large chunks of apple pie and ice cream disappear between the fat man's thick lips. Tiny droplets of vanilla ice cream coated his black mustache. Food stains patterned the shiny gray tie. Nadim was trim and athletic. He was repelled by the display of gluttony. He picked up his plastic spoon and stirred his yogurt. He spoke in a low monotone.

"There are problems, big problems. The bomb failed to detonate. Why is that?" He fixed his icy stare on the fat man's undulating chins. "Are you going to claim it was bad luck? Or were the police alerted in time to dismantle the bomb?"

Nadim's contact started to speak. Nadim silenced him with an impatient wave of his hand.

"D'Abernon is on to something," Nadim continued. "But given his present situation, he isn't in a position to do much about it— which could be a big advantage for us right *now*." He emphasized the "now" and paused.

"Whatever went wrong at the consulate does not matter anymore. The situation has changed and we will change our plans accordingly. This thing has become much bigger than we anticipated." Nadim noticed with satisfaction the look of surprise on the fat man's face.

"I received word this morning that the Egyptian and Chinese presidents and the Israeli prime minister have accepted the mayor's invitation to the gala dinner at the Wyndham Institute." Nadim watched his contact's fork clatter onto his tray. There are some things, at least, that could make the man stop eating, Nadim thought.

Nadim continued. "They will be right here, thanks to McManus and his political ambitions. He has been playing up the exhibition because he thinks it will reflect his expertise in foreign affairs and get him the Jewish, Muslim, and Asian votes. But we will turn his political maneuvering to our advantage. His distinguished guests will be sitting ducks at that dinner. Our job," he said as he stirred a spoonful of sugar in the yogurt, "is to assassinate the Egyptian president."

The fat man's jaw dropped. This was a lot more than he had bargained for.

"*And* to make it look like the work of Israeli extremists. That will end all talk of cooperation, negotiations will grind to a halt, and Israel will again be isolated." Nadim stared right at his contact, who averted his gaze.

"And furthermore," Nadim said as he continued to stare, "I know just the man for the job. If we plant the right papers on him, identifying him as an Israeli agent, and if we give him a rifle that can be traced to the Israelis ... He will, of course, be killed while trying to escape."

Nadim stood up abruptly. "You have until 3:00 p.m. tomorrow to produce the necessary papers and the gun. I'll pick you up at the usual place. And wear a different tie!" Nadim turned and left the fat man to dispose of both trays.

CHAPTER 11

Thursday, November 18, 9:30 p.m.

Ruth was alone in the townhouse she had bought thanks to the trust fund she inherited from her grandfather, Senator William J. Wyndham. She filled her glass with chilled pinot grigio, turned on the TiVo, and settled onto the sofa. She still had not watched her two-week-old television interview aired on *Sixty Minutes* in which she discussed her role in developing a thriving fashion industry in New York City. She decided to watch it because it would take her mind off the trial.

"Miss Wyndham," inquired the cheerful interviewer, "does quality fashion design have a future in the United States?"

The question seemed so inane coming on the heels of the first day of Nick's trial that Ruth realized she could not concentrate. Her mind returned to the events of her father's murder, Nick's arrest, and the horrifying details described by the forensic scientist. She turned off the television. Her meeting with Nick had gotten nowhere, and she was still angry that he wouldn't help himself or let her hire a top-notch legal team. He seemed deflated and defeated by his situation.

The phone rang.

"Hi, Ruth, it's me, Joe. I know it's late but I found something I think you should have. Can I come by and drop it off?"

"Sure, Joe," she said, glad of the distraction. "What is it?"

"It's a letter, and it's addressed to you. I'll be right there." Joe Padrone hung up.

Ruth met Joe at the front door. Her hand trembled as she took the heavy manila envelope from him. She recognized her father's decisive copperplate handwriting, and it unsettled her.

"It's his writing, all right," Padrone said. "I'd know it anywhere."

"But how—" Ruth began.

"I don't know. There are a couple of strange things about it. I found the envelope in your father's office. The police went through everything and either missed it or someone put it in the office when forensics had finished. After I testified, I returned to the Institute to check security. I noticed the envelope because a corner of it was visible behind the books."

"How odd." Ruth stared at the envelope and slowly turned it over.

"That's another thing." Padrone pointed to the back, noticing her puzzled expression. "The envelope was torn open, but the letter was inside. I tried dusting it for prints, but it's clean. The police haven't seen it, by the way. I thought you should read it first."

"I see. Thank you, Joe. Would you mind if I read this by myself?"

"Of course not. I'll give you a call tomorrow. Don't show it to anyone else. I don't want to be arrested for tampering with evidence."

Ruth closed the door behind Padrone's burly, well-wrapped figure and shivered involuntarily from the blast of cold air. She returned to the living room. Sinking into the sofa, she removed a yellow legal pad from the envelope. Her father's flowing handwriting covered each page. She leaned against the cushions and began to read:

"My dear Ruth,

"I hardly know where to start, or how I shall end this letter. I can only hope to make up with written words what I should have told you directly. I was the one responsible for the barriers between us, not you. I hope you will forgive me for not realizing that I had lost myself in abstract ideals. In so doing, I overlooked the one person who needed me, and whom I needed, the most—you."

It was nearly midnight when Ruth finished her father's letter. For the first time she understood his dedication to the Institute. He had created it with the hope that an understanding of human nature would improve society. Now Ruth finally had a clear picture of her father's motives. She picked up the letter and reread it.

Samuel Wyndham, the boy raised on Beacon Hill in Boston, had been a child during the conservative 1950s. His parents were proper Bostonian Brahmins who left him and his two younger brothers in the charge of housekeepers and governesses as Samuel's father led the demanding social and political life of a US senator. His mother devoted herself to furthering her husband's career. Both his parents had been adamant supporters of the anti-Communist crusade led by Senator Joseph McCarthy in the 1950s, and they believed that winning the war in Vietnam would be a crucial step in the ultimate defeat of the Communist threat.

The four years Samuel spent as an undergraduate at Harvard in the late 1960s introduced him to other opinions and views of the world. His study of science and the humanities convinced him of the complexities of human nature. He became aware of the way society shapes an individual's point of view, how extremes of wealth and poverty determine political choices, and the enormous role conflict and war have played in human history. He decided to pursue a graduate degree in anthropology in order to devote his life to studying the evolution of human culture and society. Much to the dismay of his conservative parents, he became involved in the civil rights movement and while in college marched against the Vietnam War. As the disagreements between Samuel and his parents escalated, Samuel wondered how man had evolved into a creature of such opposites, love and altruism on the one hand and hatred to the point of genocide on the other.

Samuel's ambition was interrupted when he was drafted into the army and sent to Vietnam. He never told Ruth about his experiences during the war, and Ruth never dared to ask, understanding that he preferred not to discuss them. Now in his letter, he did.

"It was an inferno," he wrote. "Two years of indescribable insanity. There was no way to know who our enemies were or who was on our side. I was against the war and I felt like a modern Dante descending into the depths of hell. In one battle, my division was under constant siege for seventy-seven days. I nearly went mad. Men were blown up all around us, I lost my two best friends, and the bombing never let up. Even after I returned home and began graduate school at Harvard, I was unable to shake off the memory of the war. I could no longer concentrate on my classes, it was impossible to read, and images of severed limbs and blasted bodies haunted my dreams. Finally I had to take a leave of absence."

It was Samuel's mother who told him about the private sanatorium in Connecticut, where he would get the help he needed. His father objected.

"Wyndhams don't need outsiders telling them what to do," he said. "It's a sign of weakness. Wyndhams handle their own problems." Samuel suspected that his father was more concerned with his own political future should the press get wind of his mental breakdown than the health of his son.

But Samuel's mother had her way.

"The doctors helped me a lot. They were easy to talk to. I began to read again. I was determined to understand human nature. I discovered conflicts I never knew I had. I realized that the human mind is infinitely complex and driven by forces that must be better understood if we are to survive as a species. That was the beginning of my idea for the Wyndham Institute. As my health improved, my plans became more focused, though it was sometime before I took concrete steps. When I left the hospital, I returned to Harvard and finished a degree in physical and cultural anthropology. You see, I had an idea about evolution, which was the subject of my PhD thesis. In 1974, my chance came for an important piece of research. I received a grant to travel to the Neander Valley in Germany to investigate the site where Neanderthal Man had been discovered. There I made a remarkable discovery of my own."

Ruth knew the rest of the story. Her father had unearthed hundreds of pieces of skulls and bones and, among them, enough fragments to reconstruct the partial skeleton of a young boy. His protruding brow and occipital bun combined with long leg bones convinced Samuel that Neanderthal Man and *Homo sapiens* had produced offspring together. This discovery flew in the face of the theory of human evolution prevailing at that time, which asserted that Neanderthal Man and *Homo sapiens*, the direct descendent of modern man, were distinct species that could not mate. Samuel's discovery provided the "missing link." Not the link between men and apes that scientists had sought since Darwin, and that was still being sought; Samuel's link explained the contradictions of human nature. Modern man was the problem child of the unlikely coupling of Neanderthal Man and *Homo sapiens*. As Samuel used to say, Ruth well remembered, "If you saw one of the first *Homo sapiens* wearing a business suit, you wouldn't notice him. That's how similar he was to us. But Neanderthal Man was different in crucial ways. Even on a New York subway he would stand out. Neanderthal Man lived in small, tribal groups. They stole each other's women and were incapable of forming the kind of stable societies that make progress possible. In addition, there is no evidence that Neanderthals produced works of art. That seems to be a purely human activity."

Because Neanderthal Man was less intelligent and less adaptable than *Homo sapiens* and unable to cooperate as a group, he lost out in the struggle for survival and disappeared as a species. Unlike *Homo sapiens*, Neanderthal Man never learned to channel his aggressive instincts into developing higher forms of culture. It was for this reason, Samuel theorized, that the interbreeding of these two hominids explained the conflict between tribalism and cooperation, on the one hand, and aggression and altruism, on the other, that was a key characteristic of modern man. The Neanderthal component, Wyndham concluded, was in conflict with *Homo sapiens*. It was the Mr. Hyde struggling against the Dr. Jekyll in all of us.

"The public loves a catchy phrase," Samuel wrote. "So I invented one. I called my reconstructed skeleton *Homo jekyllensis*, and it caught on. Shortly after I made my discovery, I met your mother."

Ruth put down the letter and refilled her glass. She thought fleetingly of her own meeting with Nick. It seemed as if she, as well as her father, was ill-fated in love.

Ruth picked up the letter again. Her mother, the quiet but imaginative Eileen Lathrop, had been Samuel's student during his first year of teaching in the Harvard Anthropology Department. Samuel came to appreciate her work. The first time he called on her in class she appeared embarrassed, but she recovered herself and delivered a succinct and well-reasoned refutation of his argument. He was taken aback and decided that she was a student worth watching.

And watch her he did. Surprise quickly turned to admiration and admiration to love. When he proposed marriage, she accepted at once. Samuel and Eileen were ideally suited to each other. Both were intelligent, attractive, and hard working. They shared interests, tastes, and ideals. But there was a problem: it was an unwritten rule at Harvard that professors did not marry students.

"I never cared—and never had to care—about rules, written or unwritten. Arrogance was a Wyndham birthright, and I inherited my fair share. I blithely announced my marriage to my colleagues, with no concern for their views on the matter. In so doing, I antagonized several people whose support I would soon need. Unfortunately, I didn't understand the acrimony of academic politics or the envy of my colleagues when the press had a field day with *Homo jekyllensis*. I was interviewed on television, and since I published widely on the subject, I was invited to lecture around the world. I became a media celebrity, which was simply not done if you were a Harvard professor. My marriage, together with my popular success, was enough to end my academic career. They accused me of not being a serious scholar and made it clear that I would not get tenure. The only faculty member who came to my defense was Frances Atwood, even though she disagreed about the implications of my discovery. Over the years Frances became my closest friend.

"That was it, Ruth. The time for the Wyndham Institute was ripe. I went to my two younger brothers, who directed the Wyndham Trust. I relinquished my share of the trust in return for enough capital to endow the Institute and live independently. Then I went to work. I was a man with a mission. I intended to make the Wyndham Institute an international center for the study of human evolution—evolution of mind as well as body, evolution of man himself, his brain, his civilization, his arts, and his sciences. And I did it. The Wyndham Institute is unique in the world. It is both a museum and a research center. I cut across disciplines, bringing together archaeologists, anthropologists, historians, linguists, scientists, and psychologists. The library is unsurpassed. I chose my curators from the best in each field. And I pay them well.

"I was at the top of my career when you were born, which was the most exciting event of my life. Your mother's unexpected death a few years later was devastating. Even though I had you, I shut myself off from the world. I was so consumed with my own loss that I failed to realize that your loss was even greater. In a way, you lost both parents. And that, Ruth, brings me to the present. Something has gone wrong and I'm afraid the fault is largely mine. I tried to provide an atmosphere that would encourage creative research at the Institute. I realize now that I am too much of a perfectionist. I tried to control everything. I demanded the best without recognizing to what lengths scholars would go to meet my impossibly high standards. I know now that I was unrealistic as well as unobservant. My judgment of people has obviously been flawed. That is, except for Nick. I want you to know that I am very glad you are going to marry him. He's the one who finally opened my eyes to what's been going on at the Institute. Maybe you can help him get to the bottom of it. So far, Joe and I have failed to do so, and time is not on my side. Two weeks ago, I had my annual physical. Although I had no symptoms, the doctor diagnosed pancreatic cancer and warned me that I have only a short time to live. I haven't told anyone yet. It would be detrimental to the investigation, and I still hope to get the Institute back on track. But in case something happens to me, I am writing this letter to you, outlining the facts as I know them. For a long time I refused to listen to Nick's suspicions of the curators. I didn't believe Joe either. But when I was confronted with acts of outright vandalism and with the hard evidence of theft, forgery, and ..."

Ruth had come to the last page. There was nothing else. What, she wondered, had happened? Had her father been interrupted in the middle of a sentence? It did not seem likely. She studied the binding on top of the legal pad and noticed the ripped edges of missing pages. Someone must have torn out the rest of the letter.

Why? How absurd his murder now seemed. He was going to die anyway. Whoever killed him had been desperate, just as Padrone had warned. And the murder was clearly someone at the Wyndham Institute. Tomorrow she would talk to Joe.

CHAPTER 12

"The prosecution calls Charles Dudley."

Nick had mixed feelings as he watched Charles Dudley approach the witness stand. It was day two of the trial and Dudley was the prosecution's first witness of the morning session.

Tall and thin, with straight gray hair that fell over his forehead, Lord Charles Dudley looked the perfect English country gentleman. He wore a Harris Tweed suit and brown leather brogues. The shoes hardly made a sound, which meant that Charles always seemed to be creeping up on his colleagues. Nick thought he was a master of British understatement. His manners were impeccable, and he had a slight stutter or "aristocratic hesitation," as Peter liked to call it.

Charles Dudley was the son of an earl and the younger brother of a career diplomat who was presently the British ambassador to Egypt. But Charles's life had not been as charmed as Nick believed. For it was his brother, and not Charles, who inherited the Dudley fortune. Charles had to be content with a small legacy that yielded a modest annual stipend. His salary from the Wyndham Institute was generous. But with two children attending American colleges, much of that was used up. It certainly did not cover his Bentley or the forty-five-foot yacht he kept off the coast of Maine. Nick knew his wife must control the purse strings. She entertained lavishly in their New York penthouse on tree-lined East Sixty-Fifth Street between Madison and Fifth Avenues.

Margaret Dudley was the daughter of a tradesman who owned a chain of fish-and-chips shops in the industrial cities of northern England. Nick was well aware of the social gap between her and Charles. He could tell from Margaret's makeup and her clothes. Both were overdone.

When Nick joined the staff of the Wyndham Institute, he had the impression that Charles Dudley was in favor of his appointment. Nick had expected to be a target for the hostility of the curators. He assumed that professional jealousies would be aroused by his relative youth and his sudden appointment as assistant director without an official search. He and Charles were in the same field—ancient Near Eastern and Minoan archaeology—and they had spent a great deal of time discussing problems of mutual interest. But as Nick got to know Charles better, he began to question his scholarship. Something about it nagged at Nick. He could not articulate it, but there were inconsistencies. Still, he hadn't put his finger on it.

Charles Dudley had published one of the most brilliant studies of the early city-states of Mesopotamia, the site of the dawn of civilization. The publication was based on Charles's doctoral thesis at Cambridge, which was an unusually accomplished study for such a young scholar. He demonstrated important cultural links between Mesopotamia and the pre-Aryan civilizations of Harappa and Mohenjo-Daro on the Indian subcontinent. That work had made Charles's reputation, but none of his subsequent papers, which dealt primarily with the gold objects discovered in 1922 by Sir Leonard Woolley in the royal cemeteries at Ur, had been as original. Nick considered Charles rather narrow and pedantic, lacking in the breadth of vision that had initially attracted the attention of the international scholarly community.

"Did you overhear the argument between Nicholas d'Abernon and Samuel Wyndham?" Crawford pressed Dudley.

"Er, well ..." Charles's hands twisted in his lap. "Wyndham was shouting at d'Abernon. He sounded very angry."

"Objection!" Rogers called out. "The witness is giving an opinion. He did not hear the entire argument."

Nick remembered the argument vividly. He was disappointed with Samuel's attitude, and he had not been able to make him see his point of view at all. The Institute's staff had been curious, but Nick was not going to say anything before Samuel did. Now Samuel was dead. As far as Nick was concerned the issue was better buried with him. That was another reason why Rogers refused to let him testify. Nick understood Rogers's motivation, but he could not bring himself to tell even his attorney what the argument had been about.

"How would you describe the relationship between Samuel Wyndham and Nicholas d'Abernon?" Crawford persisted.

"Well, when Nick ... uh ... Mr. d'Abernon first came to the Institute they were the best of friends. Relied on each other quite a bit—especially about administrative matters and Institute policy. Later it became clear that Nick ... er, Mr. d'Abernon ... wanted more interaction with the community and students and more transparent contact with the press. Wyndham was secretive. Never got over his treatment at Harvard as an academic. He would not allow d'Abernon to make those contacts. It was a different point of view. Then after that first meeting—"

"First meeting? Was there a second meeting?"

"No, no. I meant because of the murder. You know, Wyndham's

death." Charles Dudley hesitated. He seemed suddenly bewildered. He had lost his train of thought.

"The relationship between d'Abernon and Wyndham," Crawford prompted.

"Oh yes, quite so. Well, after the argument their relationship was rather strained. And then Wyndham seemed to be avoiding Nick … Mr. d'Abernon. There was a lot of tension between them."

"Now then, Lord Dudley," Crawford said as he switched his line of questioning, "you are considerably older than Nicholas d'Abernon, are you not?"

"I, er, yes, I suppose I am."

"How did you feel about Samuel Wyndham hiring a younger man as his assistant director? You had, after all, been on the staff for quite some time. And you are in a similar field."

"D'Abernon is very bright. Unusual really …"

Here it comes, thought Nick, the part about my ambition and opportunism.

Charles Dudley wished he had been as original and creative as a young man as Nick. Then he would not be in the mess he was in. If he had not been under so much pressure to succeed, he would never have gotten involved with Nigel Pembroke. It had happened while he was at Cambridge. His older brother was doing well in the diplomatic service, leading a glamorous life while, he, Charles, was a drone. Oh, it sounded good, the things he was doing, learning cuneiform and excavating in Iraq. But Charles knew he would never excel. Fortunately for Charles, he met Margaret. After they were married, Charles met Nigel, who was also at Cambridge and in the same field.

Nigel was continually in need of money. He was a gambler, whose aristocratic veneer masked his passion for bath houses and rough trade boys. Nigel had the flair and originality that Charles lacked. He and Nigel were out drinking in a local pub when their agreement was finalized. Nigel would write Charles's thesis in exchange for enough money to support his dissolute lifestyle.

Charles published the work under his own name and became an instant success. Nigel, meanwhile, sank into the near-oblivion of drug addiction. Charles never forgave himself for getting involved with Nigel, who continued to blackmail him. There was always the threat of exposing his fraudulent publication.

The worst of it was that Margaret knew the whole story. She found out about Nigel only after their first child was born. But she would have stayed with Charles anyway. She reveled in the title that came with her husband, *Lady* Margaret. The money, most of it, was hers, but she wanted the title for social advantage. What was the use of money without the right social connections? Margaret invariably recognized Nigel's letters. *She* was the one who paid him off. If Charles lost his reputation, *her* social life would collapse. They would both be disgraced, which did not fit in with her plans.

Lately Margaret had been accusing Charles of paranoia. He was convinced that Nick was suspicious of him. He sensed that Nick might know that he had not written the book that made him famous. Had Nick discussed the matter with Wyndham? Charles wondered. Just now, however, Charles had more important things to think about. This was his chance to make certain, reluctantly of course, that Nick would cease to be a threat.

"Yes," Charles conceded. "Nick *was* ambitious. Still is. So are most brilliant men."

"Please just answer the question." Crawford intended to leave the jury with a firm belief in Nick's overriding ambition. It was cleverly planned too. Crawford's strategy was obvious to Nick. He would take advantage of Charles's naturally aristocratic style to convey his sense of conviction. If Charles considered Nick a social upstart invading his territory, then the jury was bound to think so too. Charles was expected to know such things. It was all part of being to the manner born.

Nick watched with apprehension as his attorney rose to cross-examine Charles Dudley.

"Lord Dudley," Rogers began, "before the meeting called by Samuel Wyndham, had you known about the problems the Institute was having with its collections? The forgeries, for example?"

"No, I did not. None of those incidents occurred in my department. Every work I exhibit is fully authenticated. Each one has a legitimate provenience and a documented provenance."

"Provenience? Provenance?" Rogers was hesitating again, stopping at the wrong places. Nick was discouraged.

"Can you tell the jury what is meant by 'provenience' and 'provenance'?"

"Of course. They are the equivalent of a pedigree. Each object comes from somewhere, its place of origin. When we know the excavation history of an object, where it was found and its particular context within a site, we say it has a provenience. Ancient history is written largely from such objects, so it is crucial that we know their exact provenience. The term provenance refers to the history of ownership after the object's excavation context has been recorded. Both are necessary to insure the history, meaning, and authenticity of any ancient work."

"I see, thank you." Rogers looked at his notes. "Now, Lord Dudley, did you have any discussions with Samuel Wyndham after the meeting?"

His encounter with Wyndham flashed through Dudley's mind. He had told no one about it, of course. Did Rogers's question mean that Nick knew about the meeting? It was devastating. Nigel had stopped sending the blackmail letters to Charles at home. Instead he sent one to Wyndham, threatening to expose Charles *and* the Institute. Nigel must have been out of his mind to imagine that he could blackmail Samuel Wyndham!

Worst of all, Samuel had summoned Charles to his office. It was the day after the meeting with the curators. Charles saw the letter on the desk and recognized Nigel's handwriting. Wyndham was quiet. He fixed Charles with a stern gaze. He put on his glasses and silently reread the letter. Charles remembered the look of disapproval and disappointment and, then, of sympathy. The sympathy was the worst. He had long since become used to Margaret's snide remarks and Nigel's threats. Sympathy was something new.

"I do understand that these things can happen," Wyndham had said. "A man gets caught up in himself and his career, especially when he's young and his future is the most important thing in the world. Sometimes events seem to take over. From the sound of this Nigel, it's just as well that you published the work in your own name. After all, it's the knowledge that's important, the contribution to history and science. Not who publishes it."

Charles had breathed a sigh of relief. The old man understood. Charles was amazed, and for a moment he let down his guard and relaxed.

But Samuel Wyndham had continued. "I personally do not care whether you or Nigel or anyone else did the original work. Unfortunately, however," Samuel paused and adjusted his glasses, "other people do."

"The reputation of the Wyndham Institute is now at stake. I can forgive the personal deception, but I will never compromise the Institute. It has been my life, and I am not about to allow your youthful folly to destroy it."

Charles's heart beat faster and faster. He felt disoriented.

"You will have to do the honorable thing, Charles. I will accept nothing less than a frank public statement. You must acknowledge the true authorship of your publication. Otherwise the Institute becomes a party to blackmail. If I agree to pay Nigel even once, he will have a hold over us for life. As I see it, the only way to deal with threats of this kind is to defuse them immediately."

Charles had not said much at first. The weight of years of deception would finally be lifted from his shoulders. Nigel would never get another cent. Charles had a perverse sensation of pleasure at the thought of Margaret's chagrin when her social world collapsed around her. Everyone would know she had married a fraud. On the other hand, however, it would not do the children any good. There would certainly be publicity. Their friends would know. Charles would never again find a respectable job. He would not be allowed to direct another excavation. In short, his career would be finished and his reputation ruined.

As for Margaret, if she stayed with him she would be impossible. If she divorced him, he would have very little to live on. He tried to make Wyndham see that publishing a retraction would reflect badly on the Institute. He begged for time to think things over.

"I'm sorry, Charles," Wyndham had said. "There is no time. I want your letter of resignation on my desk tomorrow morning."

Charles broke down. He actually cried for the first time in years. Wyndham was unmoved. He stood up. The conversation was over.

Charles knew he had to find a way out. He thought of suicide then murder. It would be very convenient, he thought, if something should happen to silence Samuel Wyndham.

Dudley felt beads of perspiration on his forehead as the memory of that afternoon swept over him. After Wyndham's abrupt dismissal of him, Dudley realized that he had to find and destroy Nigel's letter. Wyndham's office was usually unlocked. Dudley watched the hallway, and when Wyndham left for a scheduled meeting with his security staff, he let himself in. He saw no one and was certain he had not been seen.

Dudley was rifling through the papers on Samuel's desk when he caught sight of the large manila envelope addressed to Ruth. Dudley thought it looked rather official. He opened it at once and read.

With each page, his apprehension grew. Surely Wyndham would tell Ruth what was going on at the Institute. Charles's anxiety increased as he skimmed Wyndham's declaration of love for Ruth, his life story, and his admiration for Nick. "Here it comes," Dudley said aloud as he read the description of Nigel's blackmail and Wyndham's decision that the only solution was for Charles to resign and confess his own deception publicly. What Wyndham had to say about the other curators was equally incriminating.

With trembling hands, Dudley removed the pages describing the curators, including himself, folded them up, and put them in his breast pocket. He stuffed the manila envelope on a shelf behind Wyndham's books and began to search for Nigel's letter. He found it at the back of the lower desk drawer.

That was when he heard footsteps. He grabbed the letter and slipped it into his pocket along with the torn pages from Samuel's letter to Ruth. Then he heard the knock at the door. Charles froze.

"It's me, Sam." Nick called out.

Charles did not answer. Nick knocked again and opened the door.

"Oh," Nick was taken aback at the sight of Dudley.

"Hi, Nick," Charles said, praying that he sounded casual. "I just came by to borrow a book."

"Where's Sam? He doesn't usually keep his door closed."

"I think he might have gone to a meeting. See you later, Nick. I've got some reading to do." Charles left with a parting nod. Later he realized that he had not been carrying a book and wondered if Nick noticed. Knowing him, he probably did, Charles thought bitterly.

"No," replied Lord Dudley to the defense attorney's question. "I did not see Wyndham again after the first meeting."

Rogers was defeated and Nick knew it.

"No further questions."

CHAPTER 13

"Ricardo Guzman Montoya, do you solemnly swear to tell the truth, the whole truth, and nothing but the truth?"

"I do."

Ricardo Guzman Montoya sat down. He was impeccably dressed in a pale-green Harvie and Hudson shirt and well-cut gray suit that emphasized his broad shoulders and narrow hips. He leaned back and looked expectantly at Crawford with dark, penetrating eyes. The touch of gray at his temples added to Montoya's air of distinction. He was forty-three years old, intelligent, cultivated, and very rich. He was the eldest son of a wealthy, landowning family in Colombia. Their close political ties with the ruling junta had proved extremely useful as well as profitable.

As curator of pre-Colombian art at the Wyndham Institute, Montoya had fostered cooperation and exchanges with the archaeological museums in Central and South America. He had been director of the Bogotá Museum for eight years before Samuel Wyndham brought him to New York. Montoya had his own private Lear jet, which he piloted to South America several times a month.

70

For the past year he had been dividing his time equally between Bogotá and New York because he was supervising an excavation jointly financed by the Wyndham Institute and the University of Bogotá.

Nick wondered how Montoya had the time to be New York's most eligible bachelor. He attended gallery openings, museum galas, first nights at the theater and opera, and publishers' parties. His name appeared regularly in gossip columns and was linked romantically to the most beautiful women in the city.

It is astounding, Nick thought to himself as Ricardo caressed his gold cigarette lighter, how much he can pack into one day. Nick did not like Montoya. There was something a little too smooth about him and not quite to be trusted. And it was not just because of the admiring glances Montoya threw Ruth's way.

For all his dislike of Montoya, however, Nick had to admit that he was the best of the few experts around on pre-Colombian archaeology. And he could discuss virtually any aspect of the field. In addition, Montoya was cultivated. He was as knowledgeable about Cicero's *Orations* as he was about Heisenberg's Principle of Uncertainty.

Montoya was one of the finest products of the European system of education. He had been sent to England at the age of twelve to attend Harrow. From there he had gone on to Cambridge, where he had received a double first—almost unheard of—in physics and archaeology. He had done his graduate work at the University of Heidelberg, the city where his maternal grandparents lived and where his mother had been born and raised. Very few people recognized the hairline scar on his left cheek for what it was, a scar that testified to his membership in a secret and exclusive dueling society at the university.

Nick never understood why Peter, who was usually critical of everyone, seemed to have a special tolerance, almost liking, for Montoya. Peter explained it with his usual cynicism. He admired the fact that Montoya was not a hypocrite. He did not try to hide his ambition or the lengths to which he would go to fulfill it.

Occasionally Montoya was in the lab when Nick dropped in. Nick knew that the dislike he felt for Montoya was mutual. He was perfectly civil, but he made it obvious that he would not go out of his way to seek Nick's company. Nick remembered when he and Peter had been talking about Peter's fish tank, of all things. Nick had remarked on the odor. The lab reeked like the Fulton Fish Market, and the ammonia on top of it pervaded the entire lab.

"Why don't you clean out the tank," Nick asked, "instead of trying to disguise the smell by mopping the place with ammonia? I would think that an animal lover like yourself would keep the tank clean. The fish stink."

Peter took this as an affront to the fish and disregarded Nick's criticism of his laboratory conditions. He laughed and launched into a diatribe on how inappropriate it was for humans to criticize animals. "No animal," Peter said, "kills and tortures other members of its own species for the sheer pleasure of it. Only men do that—and women," he added with a grin. At that moment, Montoya had poked his head around the lab door.

"Peter, my friend, I have a shipment for you to unpack." Montoya had not seen Nick. When he did, the casual tone disappeared.

"Excuse me for interrupting," he said, and he left abruptly.

"What was that all about?" Nick asked Peter. "Why can't he unpack his own shipments? Everyone else does."

Peter was amused. "Christ," he said, "the poor bastard might get a spot on his three-thousand-dollar suit or ruin his manicure."

Nick's recollection was interrupted by Crawford's next question.

"Mr. Montoya, I take it that you were at the curators' meeting called by Samuel Wyndham shortly before his death?" The slight sneer that had been so noticeable in Sinclair Crawford's voice when he questioned Peter Ryan had completely disappeared. In Nick's view, Montoya was the kind of man Crawford would respect. For all the differences between them, the one quintessentially European and the other top-drawer American, there was a bond forged by wealth and class. Both dressed well, and both lived well. They could probably spend an agreeable time together discussing the relative merits of a 1962 Chateau Lafitte Rothschild and a La Tâche, Nick thought with a shrug.

"Yes, I was."

"Did you have any idea that the Institute was faced with such serious problems?"

"No. No, I had no idea." That was the correct response, Montoya assured himself. Of course I knew what was happening, he thought to himself. I would have been an idiot not to. The look on Jorn Hill's face said it all. So did Dudley's. And Lillian Nakamura's visits from the disreputable Charlie Wei clinched it. That things are never what they seem was a lesson Montoya had learned as a child.

He was, he knew, more observant than most people. He had had to be. How old was he when he discovered the double life his grandparents led? It was difficult to remember exactly, but he knew that children like himself were remarkably aware even if they did not understand the implications of what they saw.

It had happened a few years before Ricardo was sent to school in England. He must have been seven or eight at the time. He decided to explore the network of cellars under the large house on the coast where his family spent the early part of every summer. At the back of the basement, hidden by a storage area, Ricardo noticed a door that was slightly ajar. He pulled it open. It took him a moment to adjust to the dark, and then he saw a pair of luminous eyes staring at him from a corner of the hidden room. He remembered his panic. He stood rooted to the spot, hardly daring to breathe. His heart pounded furiously and he felt the blood rushing to his ears. When he heard the loud, plaintive Meeee-ooooow, he relaxed at once.

He found a switch and flicked on a light. Right in front of him was a large black cat with wide yellow eyes. It peered at him from behind an old mattress propped against the far wall. Ricardo was curious. He edged his way to the mattress, avoiding old paint cans and cardboard boxes and brushing aside cobwebs. Suddenly, the cat disappeared. When Ricardo moved the mattress aside, he saw another small door. He had to stoop to go through it. It led to another room and another light switch.

Ricardo found himself in a large space furnished with a bed, an easy chair, a desk, a table and two wooden chairs, a bookcase, a small gas refrigerator, and a portable kerosene stove. That was how he discovered that his grandparents had run an underground railway for European refugees who wanted to settle in South America. It was not until years later that he realized the fugitives were fleeing Germany, that they were, in fact, Nazis who had escaped from Germany after World War II.

When Ricardo was older, his parents explained everything to him: "Hitler was ahead of his time," they said. "He understood what very few people have the courage to admit. Humanity is facing a crisis. If mankind is to survive, the superior races will have to protect themselves. We must eliminate the masses of inferior people who threaten to destroy our civilization. They pointed out that even though during the war the official policy of the British government had been anti-Nazi, some of the leading aristocrats had supported Hitler. His parents reminded him that no less a personage than the Duke of Windsor and his American wife had met with Hitler. In fact, they said, the basement safe house built and furnished by his grandparents was part of a much larger network. And many members of the English aristocracy were involved in it. "Don't take our word for it," they had said. "Read what others say."

For the next few years, Ricardo immersed himself in the writings of Houston Stewart Chamberlain, Oswald Mosely, Charles Lindberg, Alfred Rosenberg, and Adolf Hitler. Their arguments made perfect sense to Ricardo. He had grown up in a world where the division between the rich and educated on the one hand and the poor and illiterate on the other was pronounced. It seemed to him that two distinct races were involved. The short, squat Colombian peasants had nothing in common with people like himself. They were out of a different century and belonged to an impoverished, degenerate culture.

When Ricardo arrived in New York to assume his new position at the Wyndham Institute, he was struck by the same disparity between rich and poor, educated and illiterate. The reality of city life seemed to him to be in glaring contrast to the token liberalism preached by so many of the fashionable people he met. Ricardo kept his views to himself. He was, after all, a foreigner and an outsider. But he was also a careful observer. He watched with satisfaction as the mood of the United States became increasingly conservative.

Throughout his entire life, Ricardo stood up for the rights and privileges of his class as his parents had hoped he would. That was the only morality he understood and the only morality he practiced. When inflation began taking a heavy toll on his family's assets, he used his position and connections to take advantage of the periodic deflations that crippled less fortunate Colombians. One of his cousins was deputy minister of finance, and Ricardo was quietly informed whenever the peso was about to be devalued. He would then remove pesos from the country, change them into dollars, and reexchange them when the peso stabilized at a lower rate.

Ricardo found other ways to bolster the family fortunes. He carried on a brisk trade in smuggling pre-Colombian artifacts, authentic as well as forged, out of South America. The demand for pre-Colombian art had escalated tremendously since the 1960s and there were not enough genuine objects to satisfy all the collectors. It was like the demand for Beaujolais, he thought. More bottles of that wine were sold in England alone than were produced in France.

In recent years, Ricardo had made use of his political connections to smuggle heroin into the United States. This was the most lucrative of all his ventures and the one that fit in perfectly with his social philosophy. In his opinion, the condemnation of the drug trade was ludicrous. If people were stupid enough to poison themselves, they deserved to die. Drugs killed off the weak, the incompetent, the unfit—in short, the dregs of society. In doing so, the drug trade provided a service that society at large was too cowardly to perform itself. And what's more, Ricardo reaped a large profit from it.

Montoya wished that the prosecutor would get to the point. He was dying for a cigarette.

Crawford was thinking tactics. There was no point in prolonging his questioning of Montoya. He might just as well go in for the kill now and let Rogers try to pick up the pieces.

"Mr. Montoya, I gather that you were in your office at the Institute on the night that Samuel Wyndham was murdered. Is that correct?"

"Yes."

"Can you tell us where your office is in relation to the office of Nicholas d'Abernon?"

"My office is directly across the hall from his."

"Did you hear anyone enter Mr. d'Abernon's office on that night?"

"Yes. Samuel went into d'Abernon's office. I know it was Samuel because he stopped by my office to see how I was getting on with the catalogue for a forthcoming exhibition of Aztec jewelry."

"Did you hear anyone enter Mr. d'Abernon's office before or after Mr. Wyndham?"

"No. I did not. And my door was open." That should do it, Montoya thought.

The judge ordered silence.

The conclusion was self-evident. If no one else had entered d'Abernon's office except Samuel Wyndham, no one but Nick could have killed Samuel Wyndham. Montoya would never reveal the fact that someone else *did* enter Nick's office, or who that person was. Montoya was planning how best to profit from this knowledge.

"Thank you, Mr. Montoya. No further questions."

Court was adjourned until 2:00 p.m.

As Montoya left the courtroom, he decided that he had accomplished quite a lot. And all before lunch.

CHAPTER 14

J oe Padrone waited for Ruth after the adjournment. "Let's go to lunch," he said. "You need a break, and I know just the place."

Ruth had to smile in spite of herself. Joe's "places" were everywhere. No one loved to eat like Joe. For as long as she could remember, when her father was too busy to spend time with her, Joe would take her out for a meal.

"All right," she said. "But I'm not very hungry. You'll have to eat for two."

"Don't I always?" He smiled. "The fashion business is not good for your appetite. Women shouldn't be so thin. They need a little padding."

"I can't very well be fat when my models are so thin you can barely see them." Fashion seemed miles away to Ruth. "Listen, Joe," she was suddenly serious. "I want you to do me a favor."

"Anything."

"I want you to see Nick this evening, after the recess, and talk to him."

"Look, Ruth," Padrone said in dead earnest, "I know this is difficult. I loved your father as if I were his own son. I advise you to give it up and let Nick go. He's no good. He was after your father's money and the prestige of the Wyndham Institute."

Padrone had never liked Nick. He thought of him as a usurper of Samuel's position. Padrone had the old-fashioned cop's distrust of intellectuals. Except for Samuel, of course. He had practically been the father Padrone had never had. And he was older. Nick was young and attractive. It occurred to Padrone that he might be jealous of Nick. But even so, Padrone assured himself, finding Samuel murdered in Nick's office and Nick standing over him with the ax put an end to any doubts. And Padrone would never again envy Nick. He wouldn't want to be in his shoes right now. The murder scene still haunted him.

"No," Ruth protested, "I don't believe Nick is guilty. And I really do want you to talk to him. I have to know about the argument he had with my father. It could give us a clue to the real murderer."

"But the argument has been covered in court, in Peter Ryan's testimony as well as in Dudley's. It's pretty clear what d'Abernon was after."

"Don't you see? That's just it. It's not clear at all," Ruth persisted. "Peter only described what my father said, and Dudley only heard shouting. They didn't mention a single word of what the argument was about. And another thing, do you remember that letter you brought me last night? From my father? I have read it over and over. I think you should read it too."

Ruth drew the bulky envelope from her tote bag and handed it to Padrone. "This will prove how much my father trusted Nick."

"My father was going to die, Joe. He had cancer. The doctors gave him only a few months to live, but ..." Ruth saw Padrone's shocked expression and continued before he could interrupt. "He was afraid that something might happen to him first. He finally realized that you and Nick were right about the Institute. It wasn't just the smashed statues that alarmed him. He was about to tell me what it was when the letter broke off. There's something strange about the letter, Joe. It's not signed, and it ends in the middle of a sentence and pages are ripped out. Obviously someone took part of it. And why was it stuffed behind the books? It must have been put there in a hurry by whoever took the missing pages."

"My God, poor Samuel! Why didn't he tell anyone?" Padrone was taken aback. "Let me read the letter first, and then I'll talk to Nick. But don't expect much to come of it."

"Thank you. I can always count on you."

"On one condition," Padrone added. "On the condition that you promise to eat a hearty lunch and stop brooding."

Ruth laughed out loud for the first time since her father's death. "I'll agree to the first half."

Padrone whisked Ruth out a back door to avoid reporters and photographers.

His "place" turned out to be a discreet Italian restaurant three blocks from the courthouse with red-and-white checked tablecloths. The atmosphere was enhanced by a space at the back where the regulars played bocce ball on a strip of Astroturf. As Ruth and Padrone entered, they saw Charles and Margaret Dudley deep in conversation at a small corner table under a faded, slightly pink photograph of the Leaning Tower of Pisa. The maître d' led Ruth and Joe to a secluded alcove.

"This is my favorite table," Padrone said. "He saves it for me whenever I'm in the neighborhood."

Padrone realized that Ruth was still preoccupied with the trial. He ordered her a glass of Brunello di Montalcino, hoping it would help her relax, and a double Grey Goose vodka martini straight up with an olive for himself. Gradually Ruth began to mellow.

She had to smile as she watched Joe pile up a mountain of mussel shells. Mussels in white wine with Italian garlic bread had always been a favorite of his. Padrone was a man of prodigious palate. He had an indomitable capacity for turning off his problems and devoting his full attention to the consumption of food.

Ruth contented herself with a salad and a small bowl of minestrone.

"You know," Padrone glanced past Ruth at the table occupied by the Dudleys, "Lord Charles and Lady Margaret are having a heated discussion. The lady has a *most* unladylike scowl on her face."

Margaret Dudley was in her early fifties and did her level best to avoid looking her age. She spent a considerable amount of time on treadmills, stair masters, and stationary bicycles. Her weekly hairdresser appointments kept the roots of her hair the same golden hue as the ends. Her face had the masklike quality of having been lifted and Botoxed one too many times. She wore her hemlines a shade too high and her necklines a shade too low. Ruth always had to suppress the urge to adjust Margaret's clothing. Lately, however, Margaret had taken care to cover her arms, since they were the first to go on women of a certain age.

"Well, Charles," Margaret said as she beamed forth a deadly radiance, "you *are* lucky that Samuel died before he discovered Nigel was blackmailing you. His last letter did, after all, threaten to expose you." Margaret did not notice her husband's slight grimace.

"Surely," he replied, "you mean that *you*, not I, are the lucky one." He realized with relief that she suspected nothing of his last encounter with Wyndham or that Nigel had sent a letter directly to the Institute. This is going to be another of those luncheons, he thought.

"What would you do," he said aloud, "with me in disgrace? No more bridge games, no more teas or supper parties, and definitely no more invitations the Hamptons, Glyndbourne, Cowes, or Ascot."

Charles watched Margaret in disgust as she picked at her arugula salad. Poor Margaret, he told himself. She never could get over her belief that eating everything on one's plate was lower class. Try as he might, Charles was unable to persuade her that *he* had been taught by his nanny to eat what was put in front of him.

"Nonsense, Charles," Margaret would snap. "You just want to make a fool of me."

As a young woman, Margaret had been beautiful. Charles would admit that. And her manners had been of little importance to him. His family had not been thrilled when he married her, and they had breathed a collective sigh of relief when the newlyweds moved to the United States. And Margaret *had* stayed with Charles even though she knew about his relationship with Nigel. She knew about the Cambridge "boys" and what she called their "sordid little games" from the beginning. She never let Charles forget that Nigel wrote his thesis.

"Your performance in court, darling, was like your performance in bed," said Margaret with another halfhearted stab at her salad. "Rather limp. If you had any balls at all, I would be tempted to think *you* killed Samuel."

"You express yourself with such refinement, my dear." Charles noticed that a piece of arugula had caught between her two front teeth. It looked settled in, framed by an array of yellowing rectangles and two shiny red lips. He hated the glossy lipstick that did not come off when she ate. Charles smiled to himself and thought how ironic it was that so small a detail could jar the configuration of a face. He conjured up a fleeting image of Margaret's ritual self-embalming as she prepared for public appearances: leaning back on the recliner, her face packed in mud, her hair in curlers, each hand out to the side dipped in a manicure basin.

"*Your* performances are so studied. They lack spontaneity," Charles observed. "Just like your makeup."

"Really, Charles, how could you have let yourself get into this impossible position with Nigel? Do you realize the effect it will have on the children if it comes out in court? It will be in all the papers."

"How unfortunate for your social position."

"If even a hint of your slimy past is exposed, so help me, I will leave you. And then where will you be?"

"Oh, I don't think you would, you know."

"I certainly would. I'd divorce you!"

"No, you wouldn't, my dear. Titles don't pass with divorce. But scandals pass with titles."

Margaret smiled radiantly as Joe and Ruth stopped by their table on the way out of the restaurant. "How *are* you darlings?" Margaret inquired with forced sincerity. "You are being *so* brave, Ruth. I don't believe for a moment that Nick is guilty. And neither does Charles, of course. We are keeping our fingers crossed."

"Thank you," said Ruth softly. She made a supreme effort to control her impulse to laugh out loud.

"Lord Charles, Lady Margaret." Padrone nodded. "Come on, Ruth. We have to be on our way."

CHAPTER 15

Friday, November 19, 1:58 p.m.

Padrone left Ruth at the entrance to the courthouse. He had spotted one of his pals from the DA's office and wanted to do some nosing about on his own. Ruth was glad Joe had persuaded her to join him for lunch. She felt much better for it. The Padrone magic had worked again.

Ruth entered the building and paused to gather her resolve. She squared her shoulders, took a deep breath, and headed up the large stone staircase. She saw Lillian Nakamura on the landing. Ruth had always admired Lillian. She admired her as an intelligent, attractive woman who had made it to the top of the competitive, male-dominated museum world. She considered Lillian a friend, not a close one, but a friend nevertheless. But for the last year, ever since Nick arrived at the Institute, Ruth sensed a strain in their relationship.

"Lillian," she called out, trying to sound cheerful.

Lillian turned and waited for Ruth to catch up.

God, thought Ruth, she looks like a cornered cat. I wonder why.

"Well, well, young Miss Wyndham," said Lillian with an

unaccustomed edge to her voice. "Perhaps you now realize how foolish it is to be involved with ambitious young men." She turned on her heels and hurried away, leaving Ruth dumbfounded.

What brought that on? Ruth wondered. I guess the strain of the trial has broken Lillian's cool exterior.

Ruth proceeded down the corridor toward the courtroom. Lillian was the next witness. Clearly she was not going to be helpful to Nick's case. Ruth wondered why.

Slowly and deliberately Lillian approached the witness box. She wore a conservative Chanel suit of soft gray wool. The skirt was pleated, and the jacket trimmed with black braiding. The collar of her pale-blue silk blouse was tied with a flowing bow and her long black hair was pulled back from her delicate, oval face in a chignon. The professional and sophisticated impression Lillian hoped to make on the jury was at odds with her chaotic memories.

Lillian's every muscle was tense. She felt as if her entire life were on trial, that everything she had worked for would collapse around her with one misstep, one misplaced word. To have her reputation and self-esteem tied up with Nick d'Abernon once again was more than she could bear.

She entered the witness box and glanced quickly at Nick. She raised her right hand and swore to tell the truth.

Nick leaned forward, his elbows propped on the table, his chin resting on the back of his hands. He stared vacantly.

Lillian remembered seeing Nick like that once before. He had been sitting at her dressing table. From her bed she had caught his vacant expression in the mirror. A moment later he stood up, gazed briefly at her, and walked out of her life. That was the last time Lillian had seen Nick until he arrived at the Wyndham Institute ten years later.

She had loved Nick with a passion that astonished and frightened her. She had wanted only to please him and had tried to do so in every way she could. And she had turned him from a handsome, quiet boy into a man. Lillian never told anyone of her grief over losing Nick. Her friends would have said that she was a fool to be involved with a man fifteen years her junior. Her Japanese family would have been appalled that she had allowed herself to fall in love with a Caucasian.

From the time she had been a little girl, Lillian was repeatedly warned to distrust Americans. Her parents had never recovered from being interned during World War II. They were second-generation Japanese living in Seattle, and they spoke fluent English. Her father had played football in high school. Her mother entertained family and neighbors every Thanksgiving with turkey, sweet potatoes, cranberry sauce, and pumpkin pie. After her parents married, they took over the small but prosperous business making radio equipment that had been established by Lillian's grandfather. Then everything ground to a halt in 1942 when the Nakamuras were forced out of their suburban home and moved to a bleak, cheerless internment camp for Japanese Americans. Mr. and Mrs. Nakamura had left their factory in the hands of their lawyer.

For the duration of the war, Lillian's parents had lived in one small room, with each dreary day an endless, pointless monotony. Mrs. Nakamura watched her husband's physical and mental states decline. At first he could not believe what had happened. Eventually his disbelief turned to rage and hatred. But he had nowhere to vent his anger. He was powerless to help either himself or his wife, and because of his impotence, he turned his rage against himself. It slowly ate away at him. By the time the Nakamuras were released from internment, Mr. Nakamura was a shadow of the man he had been.

The Nakamuras returned to Seattle. Their lawyer had taken advantage of their absence to strip their factory of its assets. They were left with a heavily mortgaged building and decrepit, out-of-date machinery. The people who had rented their house had allowed it to fall into disrepair. Mrs. Nakamura decided to sell everything and move to Phoenix, where the Arizona weather was better for her husband's health. With the meager proceeds from the sale she was able to buy a small nursery and a bungalow.

Sixteen years later Lillian was born, an only child to a couple whose only real joy was her and her completely unexpected arrival. She remembered her father tending the plants. It was the one activity that still gave him pleasure, and he had been a marvelous teacher about everything involved in the cultivation of plants and flowers.

The sound of Lillian's voice jolted Nick back to reality. He still loved the way she spoke. Her tone could be so gentle and soft. He remembered the first time he heard her lecture. He was a graduate student at Stanford, and Lillian Nakamura taught a course on ancient civilizations of the Far East. He was charmed by her at once—perhaps even awed. She was an excellent teacher who involved her students in the subject matter. At the same time, however, she always managed to seem slightly aloof and intimidating. An unspoken boundary separated her professional life from her personal life. Nick was the only person who succeeded in crossing that boundary.

He was strolling across campus late one chilly November afternoon when a young man on a bicycle nearly ran into him. Nick shouted after the rider, who turned around and grinned idiotically. Not watching where he was going, the rider careened into Lillian Nakamura coming from the opposite direction, and both fell to the ground. Nick rushed to help Lillian, who was holding her ankle and rocking back and forth. She was in pain and Nick saw that tears were streaming silently down her cheeks. Nick knelt beside her and dried her tears with his handkerchief.

"Thank you," she said. "I'm okay now. Just a little bruised. I think my ankle is twisted."

Nick helped her up. She winced when she put weight on her foot.

"Here, let me give you a hand." Nick put his arm around her waist. She barely came up to his shoulder. They made their way to the bike rider who lay on his back waving his arms and legs with the same idiotic grin on his face.

"He must be stoned out of his mind," said Nick. "And he doesn't have a scratch on him. I say let's leave him where he is and let campus security pick him up."

Lillian asked Nick to help her home. When they arrived at her house, she offered him a cup of tea. Her living room was warm and cozy after the chill air. The walls were decorated with colorful Japanese prints, and a horizontal scroll illustrating a scene from the classic Japanese *Tale of Genji* stretched across the wall behind the dark-red velvet sofa. On the black lacquered coffee table were several intricately carved Netsuke figurines. One caught Nick's eye. It was the smiling, rotund figure of Hotei, the Japanese progenitor of good fortune, reclining on a sack filled with treasure. Nick sat Lillian down. "Just tell me where the tea is," he said. "I'll do the rest." And he had. He made a pot of green tea, which he served in small, porcelain tea cups. Lillian raised hers with a smile. "Cheers," she said. And they began talking.

Before long, despite the gap in their ages, the professor-student barrier disappeared.

"How about dinner?" Nick proposed. "It's the least I can do for a poor invalid." He overruled Lillian's protests. "I'll be back in a few minutes."

While Nick shopped for dinner, Lillian realized how much she was enjoying the company of the thoughtful young man who had rescued her. He returned with two large brown grocery bags.

"Relax," he said. "Dinner will be ready in no time."

But Lillian was curious. She hobbled into the kitchen and sat down to watch Nick's preparations. He poured two glasses of chilled Sancerre, unpacked the rest of the groceries, and went to work.

"My mother," he explained, "taught me that if you like to eat you better learn to cook. We started with desserts and moved backward through the courses as my taste developed. I was probably the only teenager in Aspen who liked goat cheese and gazpacho."

Dinner was a success. Nick made lemon chicken, stir-fried broccoli, and a green salad with a raspberry mustard vinaigrette. He was, Lillian decided, a most unusual young man. He sat down and raised his glass. "To bicycle accidents," he said with a grin. He looked straight into her eyes and she found his gaze and warm smile immensely reassuring. Lillian dropped her guard and began to relax. Her usual reserve melted away.

It seemed the most natural thing in the world when Nick walked around to Lillian's side of the table, lifted her up in his arms, and carried her upstairs to the bedroom. He put her down gently on the bed and touched his lips to her forehead. The moment she felt his lips, Lillian knew what would happen next and how much she wanted it. She lay completely still, scarcely daring to breathe, willing Nick to caress her.

Nick looked longingly at her. She was lovely. Her heavily lashed eyes were shut, her lips full and slightly open, her cheeks flushed.

Lillian opened her eyes and smiled. She raised her delicate arms to Nick's shoulders and pulled him to her with a force that took him completely by surprise. Her lips met his.

Nick undid the buttons of her blouse. He kissed her small, firm breasts as he felt Lillian unbuckle his belt.

For the next few months Nick was happier than he ever thought possible. Each day he awoke with a feeling of delirious exuberance. It was a while before Nick realized and reluctantly accepted that something had happened. It began with a change in Lillian's expression when they met unexpectedly on campus. She struck him as wary and apprehensive.

Lillian hardly understood it herself. She had been so happy with Nick at first. But no matter how hard she tried, she could not quell the suspicion and distrust that gradually overtook her. Again and again she heard her father warn her in his faint, shattered voice. "Never trust Americans. They are spoiled children. They take what they want, use it up, and then discard it."

Lillian began to notice that the female students were invariably attracted to Nick. She became convinced that it was only a matter of time before he left her for one of them. She was older than Nick, and she was Japanese. She was distracted and confused by conflicting emotions. Her jealousy could be paralyzing, but at the same time, she knew she loved him.

One night when Nick was in her kitchen preparing dinner, Lillian accused him of having an affair with someone else. He was dumbstruck. Despite all his efforts to reassure her, he had clearly failed. He knew how troubled she was by their age difference and different backgrounds. Nick had tried to calm her fears, never suspecting that they were impervious to reason. He could tell by the way Lillian looked at him that she had made up her mind to end their romance.

Lillian's past defeated them both. Gradually she withdrew from Nick and drifted back to her old friends and casual lovers. None of them would ever have the same power over her emotions that Nick had. She would be safe.

Several months later, when Lillian opened her front door, she was surprised to find Nick standing there. The pleading look in his eyes and sheepish grin threw her off balance and brought back a rush of her old feelings for him. Well, she thought, this visit might be a good thing after all. It will convince him that we have no future together.

"Come in," she said. "I have some company. You might enjoy

yourself." Lillian *was* beautiful; Nick had almost forgotten how beautiful. She wore a turquoise kimono embroidered with gold and silver chrysanthemums. Her hair fell loosely around her shoulders. She led Nick into the living room.

He didn't know anyone there. Lillian introduced him to a few of the guests, and he followed her into the kitchen, where an elaborate potluck dinner was spread out. She poured Nick a glass of wine as he sampled a few hors d'oeuvres.

Back in the living room, Nick settled himself on the sofa and listened to a girl with long blonde hair describe her experiences with aromatherapy. He felt very distant from both her and the young man in thin, steel-framed glasses, who gazed raptly at her. His attention wandered. He caught sight of Lillian across the room. She was deep in conversation with an older man, who turned to the dark-haired woman next to him. He whispered something to her, and the three of them headed upstairs.

The young blonde girl tapped Nick's arm. "Here," she said with a smile. "Try this; it will cheer you up." She handed him a joint, and Nick inhaled it gratefully. He was ill at ease and held the smoke in his lungs, hoping it would calm him down. After inhaling again, he passed on the joint. The blonde stared at him. "Are you okay?"

Before he could reply, the smoke lifted him into its embrace. He felt light-headed but serene. "I'm fine. Better every minute." He could not help but notice her soft blonde hair, blue eyes, and long, slender legs. He kissed her on the lips. She took his hand and drew him from the sofa toward the stairs.

The scene in Lillian's guest room came as a shock. The bed had been pushed into a corner and the floor was lined with mattresses. Music and smoke filled the air. The room had become one huge bed covered with naked bodies. A wave of revulsion flooded over Nick. The blonde girl was clearly turned on. She touched Nick again, but he pushed her aside.

One thought penetrated Nick's marijuana haze: where was Lillian? His mind suddenly cleared. What did all this have to do with love, he wondered, with the passion he and Lillian once shared? He bolted from the room, determined to find her. He rushed across the hall and pushed open the bedroom door. There was Lillian, naked and kneeling on the bed. Beneath her was the man she had whispered to downstairs. Her kimono lay discarded on the floor. The dark-haired woman sat on the bed, propped up against the headboard, watching the lovers. Lillian's hair fell over her shoulders, partially hiding her face. But Nick knew exactly what she was doing. She had done it to him, and the look on the man's face expressed the same intense pleasure Nick remembered so well. He was overcome by a powerful jealousy and trembled uncontrollably. He grabbed Lillian and lifted her from the bed.

The man beneath her sprang up. After one glance at Nick's chalk-white face, he fled, dragging the young woman with him. Nick pushed Lillian onto the bed. He slumped down on the stool in front of her dressing table, buried his head in his hands, and began to sob. After a few moments he raised his head and stared at Lillian. It was the most ghastly end to something he had believed perfect. Without a word he rose and strode from the room. He left the house and Lillian's life forever. Or so he thought.

After Nick's departure, Lillian devoted herself to work with an even greater intensity than before. She was determined to make up for the failure of her private life by proving herself professionally. She would reach the top, and from the safety of that vantage point, she would look down on her colleagues and the rest of the world.

Lillian was bright, industrious, and well equipped to take advantage of the new opportunities opening up to women. She was also willing to be unscrupulous. Lillian rose like a cork in water.

When Samuel Wyndham asked her to head the Department of

Far Eastern Art at the Institute, her most cherished dreams seemed fulfilled. As a result of her brilliance, ambition, and willpower, she found herself accepting one of the most prestigious positions in her field. Samuel Wyndham had the means to develop the best collections possible, and his research library was without parallel. He promised Lillian a free hand and ample funds. She looked forward to making the department the best in the country, maybe even in the world. And the next step would be succeeding Wyndham as director of the Institute. She pursued her goal with unrelenting single-mindedness. But she could not have done it without the assistance of one invaluable contact, Charlie Wei.

Charlie Wei approached Lillian shortly after her arrival at the Institute. He had made it his business to find out everything about Lillian long before she stepped off the plane at Kennedy Airport. From what he learned, he decided that they would be perfect partners.

Charlie was born in Shanghai in 1945, although the exact date varied according to which passport he used. His parents had been followers of Mao Zedong and both died when Charlie was four. They fought against Chiang Kia-shek, now known as Jian Jieshi, and his supporters, the Guomindang. On mainland China, they were remembered as heroes, which had proved of inestimable value to Charlie. He was raised by his only surviving relative, a distant cousin in Hong Kong. His cousin ran an antique shop and was not eager to have a young boy on his hands. But as Charlie grew up, his cousin realized that he had an eye for art and was an exceptional salesman. By the time Charlie's cousin died, Charlie was an expert on Far Eastern art and antiquities. He also had the necessary contacts for smuggling ancient art from mainland China to Hong Kong for sale in the West.

The old man left his business to Charlie, who sold it and used the money to emigrate to London. There he set himself up in a modest antique shop on Fulham Road. At a bar in Soho, he met Simon Grunewald, an investment banker who traveled regularly between London and New York. Simon was cultivated and very wealthy. He also collected Far Eastern art. He and Charlie became lovers, and Simon agreed to finance Charlie over a period of five years. Charlie knew he wouldn't need five years, but it was a nice cushion. Within a year his shop became a gallery and moved to Bond Street, and two years later Charlie followed Simon to New York with enough capital to open a branch of his business on East Fifty-Seventh Street.

Charlie had excellent sources. Obtaining the objects was no problem. Selling them could be. He needed a place like the Wyndham Institute and a curator like Lillian Nakamura to vouch for him, authenticate his pieces, and legitimize his operations.

Through a contact in New York Charlie wangled an invitation to the reception in honor of Lillian's appointment at the Wyndham Institute. "I have some objects that might interest you," Charlie said when he and Lillian had a moment alone away from the crowd. "It would be quite a coup for the Wyndham Institute to acquire them."

The sudden narrowing of Lillian's eyes told Charlie he had guessed correctly. "They are from the imperial tombs in the west," he said. She knew exactly which excavation he was referring to. "The large bronze cauldrons," he added. "I can, of course, arrange for the right contacts and papers for their legal entry into this country."

Lillian invited Charlie to lunch the following day. By the time coffee was served, they had reached an agreement: Charlie would provide the objects and the legal papers. Lillian would authenticate them, arrange for their purchase by the Institute, and take care of the provenance. Charlie would deposit substantial sums of money in a numbered Swiss bank account for Lillian.

"No, Mr. Crawford," Lillian replied, "I did not hear the argument between Mr. d'Abernon and Samuel Wyndham. My office is on another floor. But everyone knew it was about the future directorship of the Institute."

Oh, did they? Nick said bitterly to himself.

"Objection, Your Honor!" Chris Rogers jumped to his feet. "Conjecture and hearsay."

"Objection sustained."

"Very well," sighed Sinclair Crawford with affected weariness. "Let me begin again. Miss Nakamura, was it not the general opinion of the Institute's staff that Nicholas d'Abernon was going to take over the directorship when Samuel Wyndham retired?"

"General opinion is not evidence," objected Rogers.

"Overruled. I will allow the witness to answer."

"Yes, it was." Lillian paused. "And his daughter as well."

"Objection, Your Honor. I would like the last remark stricken from the record."

Nick recognized the envy in Lillian's tone. He realized that she was out to get Ruth as well as him. For the first time it was clear to him that Lillian's ambition was to become director of the Wyndham Institute.

Neither had ever alluded to their love affair. Nick assumed there was a tacit agreement between them to leave the past alone. He never discussed it with Ruth, although he now realized he had made a mistake. Lillian was his first love, his teacher in the art of romance. But that was in the past. Ruth was different.

Crawford turned to the witness. "Miss Nakamura, would you describe the situation at the Institute and why the directorship is such a desirable position?"

"Samuel Wyndham was a very rich man. He established the Wyndham Institute with his own money. Such private institutions are extremely rare nowadays. The availability of unrestricted funds and the freedom from interference, both from the government and from trustees, makes it a very attractive place to work, especially for someone who is ambitious and has vision. And it is no secret that Mr. d'Abernon is ambitious."

Nick whispered to Rogers. His lawyer rose once again with an objection. This time the judge sustained it.

Sinclair Crawford was not unhappy, however. For all Rogers's objections, Lillian Nakamura's testimony would leave the jury with the impression that Nick was a young man on the make. And that was precisely the impression he wanted the jury to have.

"Thank you, Miss Nakamura. No more questions."

Now it was Rogers's turn.

Whatever happens now, thought Nick, it can't be good. He wished Lillian would vanish into thin air.

"Miss Nakamura, would you please describe your relationship to the defendant?"

"Mr. d'Abernon is a colleague."

"But is it not true that you knew Mr. d'Abernon before coming to the Institute?"

"Yes, I met him eleven years ago at Stanford University. He was one of my graduate students."

Please stop, thought Nick. But he knew it was impossible.

"Miss Nakamura, would you tell us the nature of your relationship with the defendant during that period?"

Lillian hesitated. The memory of those months many years ago flooded over her.

"He was my lover," she said softly.

The courtroom was silent. Nick sat bolt upright. He wanted to turn and look at Ruth but was too ashamed.

Ruth was sure that everyone could hear her heart pounding. Now she understood Lillian's coldness and the forced politeness between Lillian and Nick. Why hadn't she realized it before? She knew that Lillian had taught at Stanford, and she knew that Nick had done his graduate work there. And why hadn't Nick told her? She would have preferred to hear all this from him, not this way! She sensed everyone's eyes on her. Perhaps, she thought, Joe was right. Maybe there were things about Nick that she should have known. What else didn't she know? she asked herself.

"Miss Nakamura, may I suggest to you that your testimony has been colored by your personal feelings and that you are still angry with the defendant for walking out on you as a result of your own reprehensible behavior?"

"Objection, Your Honor!" Sinclair Crawford bellowed. "The question is outrageous."

"Sustained. Mr. Rogers, you must limit yourself to the present case."

Chris Rogers had grossly overstepped himself, even he knew that. But he had managed to get his point across. Lillian Nakamura's testimony was clearly biased and untrustworthy.

"Miss Nakamura," he continued, "let's move on to less painful subjects." There was a cutting edge and a slight sneer in Rogers's voice that was worthy of Crawford. "Would you tell us what you know about the so-called irregularities at the Wyndham Institute?"

Lillian tried to pull herself together for what she knew was coming, but she found it difficult to concentrate. Chris Rogers reminded her of a mosquito buzzing around her head. She wanted to brush him away and sink into her memories.

"Miss Nakamura, I didn't hear your answer."

"Please reply to the question," ordered the judge.

Lillian looked up. "I have no knowledge of any irregularities," she said after a pause. She knew, of course, that without the irregularities that went on in her own department, her reputation would be a pale shadow of what it was.

The next question was a bombshell. "Miss Nakamura, do you mean to tell me that you and Mr. Charles Wei have not collaborated in the acquisition of smuggled and stolen objects for the Wyndham Institute? And furthermore, that you have not provided such objects with fraudulent provenances?"

The courtroom erupted. This time even Sinclair Crawford jumped to his feet. His face was purple. "I object, Your Honor. The witness is not on trial."

"Objection overruled."

That part of his argument with Samuel flashed through Nick's mind. Nick's revelation that yet another curator was undermining the Institute and his insistence that Lillian's activities be made public disturbed Samuel. He pointed out that nothing would be gained from the adverse publicity. He preferred to deal with the matter in his own way. The situation with Dudley was different, Wyndham explained. It was impossible to deal discreetly with a blackmailer. So Nick agreed to keep it quiet for the time being. He was certain that Samuel would eventually do the right thing and ask for Lillian's resignation.

"Thank you, Miss Nakamura," said Rogers. He beamed at the jury. "That will be all for the moment. But please be prepared to be recalled as a witness for the defense."

Nick watched Lillian step down slowly from the witness box. For the first time since he had known her, she appeared frail and defeated.

Chris Rogers was finally on the offensive. And he has succeeded, Nick thought. But at what cost? What was the use of any of it if he lost Ruth?

CHAPTER 16

Friday, November 19, 2:05 p.m.

N adim Tariq wrenched the steering wheel. The car swerved to the right just in time to avoid a large pothole. Damn New York and its lousy streets, he muttered. At least the traffic is light. Nadim checked the rearview mirror to make sure he wasn't being followed, downshifted into third, and moved out of the fast lane. A stream of cars passed him.

Good, he thought, still no sign of a tail. He allowed himself to relax but only a little. Relaxing was a luxury he could not afford and never had been able to afford.

Nadim Tariq was an Egyptologist with an international reputation. He had come to the Wyndham Institute from Cairo, where he had been deputy director of the Archaeological Museum. He did his work at the Institute extremely well and earned the respect of Samuel Wyndham and the other curators. But no one really knew him. He was scrupulously polite, distant, and aloof. His manner invited neither confidences nor questions. Aside from his professional qualifications, which were impressive, his personal background was shrouded in mystery.

Nadim was, in fact, not an Egyptian at all. He was a Palestinian refugee. His father had been in the import-export business, and the family lived comfortably in a large house just outside the walls of the Old City of Jerusalem. Nearby stood the King David Hotel, where the British army had its headquarters. The hotel was bombed by the Irgun, the Jewish organization dedicated to establishing the state of Israel. British officers were killed, which ended all hope for a peaceful settlement between the British, Arabs, and Jews. The situation in Jerusalem became so dangerous that Nadim's father decided to move his family to Egypt. His business was ruined. His considerable investments were reduced to nothing. The family arrived in Alexandria with little but the clothes on their backs and whatever they could carry.

Nadim's father resented his self-imposed exile. He despised the Egyptians and the job he was forced to take as an assistant manager in a shipping company. He never forgot, and he never let Nadim, who was born in Egypt, forget that they were Palestinians and that Palestinians were a superior people who had been unjustly evicted from their homeland.

The neighbors laughed at Nadim's father quite openly, and though he neither noticed nor cared, Nadim noticed *and* cared. The only way that he could come to terms with the nightmare of his family's altered existence and bear their humiliation was to dedicate himself to the cause of a Palestinian state.

The Six Days War occurred when Nadim was eleven. The ignominy of the Arab defeat made him realize how ridiculous and pathetic his family's reaction to their exile was. He recognized his father's arrogant pride in being Palestinian as a dismal failure that played into the hands of the enemy. He finally knew who the enemy was. It was not the Egyptians, and it was not any of the other Arab countries. It was Israel, backed as it was by the United States.

Nadim's awakening transformed him. He turned his tremendous

willpower, intelligence, and tenacity to the art of killing. He joined an organization dedicated to Palestinian independence and began a long course of instruction in self-defense and guerilla warfare. The rage, frustration, and hate that he had bottled up for so many years provided him with a maniacal fervor and an almost inexhaustible energy. While he was mastering the use of automatic rifles, machine guns, hand grenades, and explosives, he began to study archaeology. Ultimately, it would provide him with a perfect cover and a passport to anywhere in the world.

From the moment Nadim obtained his doctorate in Egyptology, he began to live a double life. During the day he appeared to be—and was—a hardworking, dedicated member of the staff at the Cairo Museum, a lecturer at the university, and a supervisor of museum-sponsored excavations. At night he met with his comrades to plan raids on Israeli border settlements, kidnappings, and bombings of Israeli and Jewish organizations abroad. They had recently succeeded in destroying one of the largest synagogues in Brooklyn. The rabbi had been active in the movement to bring young Palestinians and Israelis together to promote peace, something Nadim and his associates were determined to prevent.

When Nadim learned that Samuel Wyndham was looking for someone to head the Institute's Department of Egyptian Antiquities, he discussed applying for the job with his unit leader. Word came down that his presence in New York would be invaluable to the cause. He contacted the Institute and Samuel hired him.

Before Nadim's departure from Egypt, he was given access to funds in the United States that supported the Palestinian cause. He was put in touch with his New York contact and taught the code that would be his lifeline to the organization. It was only then that Nadim realized that his superior at the Cairo Museum, the small, intense, middle-aged man he had worked with for years, was a member of the same organization. This was the man to whom Nadim would send his reports and who, in turn, would pass on instructions to Nadim. Their communications were disguised in hieroglyphic inscriptions placed in the archaeological reports and exchanges that passed routinely between the Cairo Museum and the Wyndham Institute. What Nadim did *not* know was the name or whereabouts of the cell's mastermind, to whom his superior reported.

It was in response to the latest set of instructions from Cairo that Nadim was driving a rented, dark-blue Ford Taurus down the West Side Highway. Nadim automatically scanned the rearview mirror once again. Still no tail. The traffic slowed and grew heavier. Nadim looked ahead. To his right he caught a glimpse of the tall, white prow of a cruise ship. For a moment he longed to be back in Cairo with its teeming streets, mosques, souks, and sunshine, far away from the New York winters.

Skillfully weaving in and out of the traffic, Nadim edged back into the fast lane. He circumvented the cluster of cars waiting at the entrance to the dock and continued down the potholed road. He sped past several derelict, abandoned docks along the border of Tribeca, which had become fashionable since the old warehouses were transformed into artists' lofts. He turned left, following the signs to New Jersey, and flicked on his lights as he entered the Holland Tunnel.

As Nadim maneuvered the car along the narrow single lane, he reached into the pocket of his overcoat and pulled out the piece of paper on which he had written directions. To avoid detection of any kind, Nadim never used a GPS system.

When he emerged from the tunnel, Grove Street appeared on his right. Nadim turned onto it and followed the winding road until he reached Observer Highway. The light was green. He shifted into second and turned right. Ahead he saw the brilliant green copper roof of the Hoboken Terminal. He drove through the parking area toward the station and came to a stop beside the statue of Samuel Sloan, president of the Delaware, Lackawanna, and Western Railroad. The statue was the same brilliant green as the station roof.

A man with striking blond hair, dwarfed by the statue, was waiting for him. His hands were shoved deep in the pockets of his black-and-white checkered lumberman's jacket. The collar was turned up against the biting wind, and he was hopping from one foot to the other in an effort to keep warm.

Nadim reached over and opened the passenger door. The man stepped in and pulled the door shut. He blew on his hands. His long, thin face was badly pockmarked. His eyebrows and eyelashes were almost invisible and matched the limp strands of pale blond hair falling across his high forehead. His nose was bright red from the cold and drops of mucus collected on his upper lip. The man wiped them away with his sleeve.

"Five hundred thousand isn't enough," he said.

"That was the agreement," Nadim snarled.

"I've been reading the papers. And my price has doubled."

Nadim leaned across his passenger and threw open the door. A blast of freezing air whipped around them.

"Seven-fifty. Take it or get out!" he said icily.

"Okay, pal. I'll take it." The man pulled the door shut. "Fifty percent in advance."

"You'll get it the day before."

Nadim turned on the ignition. Neither spoke during the twenty-minute drive back to Manhattan. Nadim turned onto Canal Street, made a right on Broadway, and pulled up in front of Trinity Church. "Damn," he muttered under his breath.

"So where's your pal, buddy?" The blond man enjoyed Nadim's evident irritation.

At that moment the fat man Nadim had met in the cafeteria lumbered out of the church and ran awkwardly toward the car. He was carrying a parcel wrapped in brown paper under his arm. He yanked open the car door and threw himself onto the backseat.

"It's very cold," he said apologetically, handing Nadim the package.

"Here's your rifle," said Nadim. He gave the package to the blond man. "Practice with it."

"Look, pal, don't teach me my job, and I won't teach you yours."

Nadim ignored the remark. "You'll get your clothes at the pickup. You'll be posing as an FBI agent. There'll be an ID in the pocket. By Monday you'll have a plan of the Institute. Study it. You will shoot from the balcony. The place will be marked. There's an exit immediately behind your location. It's usually locked, but this time it will be open. It leads to the basement storerooms. You'll make your escape from there. A car will wait for you at the back entrance. And you won't have to worry about security guards. We are planning a few diversions to keep them occupied." Nadim paused. With the merest trace of a smile he shook the blond man's hand. "And good luck."

Surprised by Nadim's cordial manner, the fat man stared at him.

"Don't worry, pal," said the blond man. "I'm the best there is." He smiled back at Nadim and slid from the car.

Nadim watched as he strode up Broadway. He was leaning into the wind, his hands in his pockets and the package gripped tightly under one arm.

Nadim turned to the fat man. "I presume you have arranged for our friend's final exit?"

"No problem. He will be covered at all times. He won't leave the Institute alive."

"And the Israeli papers?"

"They will be 'found' by one of our men and passed on to the Egyptians."

Nadim tossed the car keys to the fat man, whose moist brown eyes widened in surprise. "Thanks for the ride," Nadim said, stepping into the street. "It's due back at the Avis on Sixty-Fourth and Third in half an hour."

CHAPTER 17

"The prosecution calls Jorn Hill."

Nick couldn't help but admire Jorn's Nordic good looks. He saw that Jorn made the same impression on the jury. Jorn was a remarkably attractive man with a craggy, tanned face and thick blond hair. His physique was good too, as Nick knew from the times they had played squash together.

"Are you familiar with exhibit A?" Sinclair Crawford asked Jorn, referring to the murder weapon.

"Yes, I am."

"Can you tell the court what it is?"

"It is a bronze ax from the palace of Knossos on Crete. It dates to the early Minoan period, around 1600 BC."

"And is it not true that you saw the defendant in the storeroom of the Institute *before* Samuel Wyndham called the meeting of the curators? And is it not true that Nicholas d'Abernon was there for the express purpose of obtaining the murder weapon?"

"Objection, Your Honor," shouted Chris Rogers, leaping to his feet. "The prosecuting attorney's remark is improper!"

"Sustained," said the judge. "Please be more circumspect in future, Mr. Crawford."

Nick noticed the beads of perspiration on Jorn's forehead. Under the circumstances, Nick had to admire Jorn's self-control.

Nick remembered the scene in the storeroom perfectly. It was located in the vast basement of the Wyndham Institute and was one of many rooms allocated to the different departments. Objects that were not on either temporary or permanent display were kept in the basement. Each curator had keys to all the department storerooms in case he or she needed a particular object for purposes of study or comparison. In order to keep track of what was removed from storage, an honor system had been devised. Whoever removed an object had to sign for it. A sheet of legal-size yellow paper was posted on the inside of each storeroom door. Borrowers signed their names, identified what they borrowed, and recorded the date and time of its removal and the date and time of its return.

When Nick unlocked the door to the Greek and Roman storeroom, he sensed another presence. Despite the pitch blackness, he knew he was not alone. But when he switched on the light, he saw no one. He decided it was his imagination. The storerooms always struck him as eerie with their massive crates and looming statues wrapped in plastic that cast shadows. The light reassured him.

He proceeded to the Aegean section of the storeroom, where he found the pre-Greek objects, including the Minoan ax he was looking for.

The Minoans inhabited the island of Crete before the arrival of the historical Greeks—known as the Dorians—on the mainland. No one knew where the Minoans came from, but Nick had a theory that their origins could be traced to early Near Eastern cultures. The Minoans were a highly developed, artistic people, who had a number of mysterious rituals. The best known was the so-called bull dance, depicted in a fresco at Knossos, which shows a girl grabbing the horns of a leaping bull, a boy somersaulting over its back, and another girl preparing to catch him as he lands. The bull, particularly its horns, was a powerful fertility symbol, and the bull dance an ancient predecessor of modern bull fights. Archaeologists believed that the double-headed ax was used for bull sacrifice.

Nick wanted to compare two Minoan axes that had been recently acquired by the Institute with several ancient Near Eastern axes belonging to his own department. He had one in his office, but the other had been in storage for some time. He found the ax easily. It was in the top drawer of the large cabinet marked "Aegean and Minoan Weapons and Ritual Objects." He removed the ax and shut the drawer.

As Nick turned to sign out the ax, he saw the blond head of Jorn Hill behind an adjacent cabinet. "My God, Jorn!" Nick cried out in surprise. "You scared me!"

Jorn jumped up, a look of panic on his face.

Nick was about to ask Jorn what he was doing when he realized that Jorn was not alone. Ted Curtis, the Institute's electrical engineer, was crouched down beside Jorn. Ted dealt with the lighting systems and was highly skilled in the display and illumination of art objects. His unruly black curls were unmistakable.

By some automatic instinct of self-preservation, Nick pretended he hadn't seen Ted. Jorn was hidden from the waist down by the cabinet, but Nick knew that he was struggling to pull up his jeans.

"Good luck finding whatever you're looking for," said Nick, hoping he sounded casual. He grabbed for the doorknob and left, taking the ax with him. In his hurry, he forgot to sign it out.

When Nick calmed down and assessed what he had seen, he realized the implications. Jorn Hill, he thought. Nick couldn't believe it! The model husband with an attractive, wealthy wife and two boys aged five and seven attending a fashionable day school in

Greenwich, Connecticut. How, Nick wondered, did Ted Curtis fit into that picture? He was a good electrician, but he struck Nick as a dubious character with little education. What, Nick asked himself, could a man of Jorn's intelligence and refinement see in someone like Ted?

Jorn often asked himself the same question. For try as he might, he could not exorcise the passion that secretly ruled his life. Even as a child Jorn had the impression that destiny had played a terrible trick on him. Of course, he never told anyone about it. One didn't discuss such things in his family, certainly not with Jorn's strict, God-fearing parents. He had grown up on a farm in North Dakota. His father was a man of the soil, for whom the traditional virtues of manliness were paramount. Jorn's father came from a family of Swedish farmers that had changed their name from Hilfson to Hill. He worked from dawn to dusk and embodied the Protestant work ethic.

Jorn remembered the crushing disappointment when his father returned home at the end of each day and turned to the bottle instead of to him. Vodka. It was always vodka. To this day Jorn hated the very sight of a bottle of vodka. He remembered his mother's disgust at the dirt on his father's boots and hands when he entered her immaculate, Spartan house. She exemplified the proverb that cleanliness is next to godliness, and she attended church every Sunday to cement the relationship. Jorn and his father accompanied her. He never could shake the memory of cold, dreary Sunday mornings and the bleak chill in the church warmed only by the fiery sermons. How Jorn dreaded those sermons, constantly threatening eternal damnation and describing in terrifying detail the tortures of hell for the least infraction.

Jorn's father flew into a rage when Jorn announced that he had won a full scholarship to the University of Pennsylvania to study archaeology. It had one of the leading departments of ancient Near

Eastern archaeology in the country. Its museum attracted scholars from around the world.

"No son of mine is going to be a sissy college boy," Jorn's father roared. "Greeks and Romans were pagans! Sinners! This is all your mother's fault. She made a bookworm out of you, a fucking fairy! Farming's what you need, my boy, a good dose of the soil. Farming is for men, real men. And farming is what you're going to do." When Jorn accepted the scholarship, he knew that whatever relationship he had with his father was at an end.

Jorn was forever grateful to the professor who recognized his ability and encouraged him to pursue a graduate degree in archaeology. If only his own father had been like Heinz Groben, his dissertation advisor. Through Heinz, Jorn participated in the excavations sponsored by the University of Pennsylvania in Greece. Through him too, Jorn met his wife Elizabeth, Heinz's daughter.

Professor Groben was something of an oddity among academics, partly because he was independently wealthy. The Groben family had emigrated from Hamburg, Germany, and made its fortune in animal accessories in the previous generation. Heinz had left the family business to his sister and her children and gone into archaeology. But it was no secret that his daughter's trust fund was worth millions.

Elizabeth was raised to admire the intellect. When she met Jorn Hill in her Greek literature class, she was studying for an MA in classics and was instantly attracted to him. Not only was he brilliant, but he was handsome. His blue eyes, blond hair, and high Scandinavian cheekbones instantly captivated her, and she arranged ways to run into him after class. It hadn't been easy. Jorn was elusive. A lot of his time was unaccounted for, and Elizabeth became increasingly jealous, though she had no idea of whom or of what she was jealous. She was jealous of Jorn's time away from her.

Finally he succumbed. They were married in a quiet ceremony

in a suburb of Philadelphia. Heinz Groben was thrilled. There was nothing he would not do for his protégé and son-in-law.

Thinking about his family gave Jorn strength. It was with them in mind, rather than Ted, that he answered Crawford's question about the ax.

"Yes," Jorn replied. "Nick came into the storeroom for the Minoan ax. I was there at the time."

Clamor in the courtroom.

The judge called for order.

"Is it not true," persisted Crawford, "that Nicholas d'Abernon failed to follow the system for signing objects out of the storeroom? That in fact he did not sign out the ax?"

"That is correct," stated Jorn Hill.

"No more questions."

Nick had never felt so defeated, nor so betrayed. He and Jorn had been friends. He, Nick, had been willing to overlook the encounter in the storeroom. Now Jorn was turning it against him.

Chris Rogers rose to cross-examine. He asked Jorn about the Mycenaean mask that Samuel Wyndham had exposed as a forgery during the curators' meeting. "Did you know that mask was forged? It did, after all, come from your department."

Of course Jorn had known. He remembered the meeting perfectly. He was shocked to see the mask lying on the table in front of Samuel Wyndham. He was certain he had been found out and that his career was over. Fortunately he had not betrayed his guilty panic. And he soon realized that Wyndham had no idea who substituted the forgery. It was a good one too, Jorn knew. Only a few experts would have suspected the substitution. Jorn thought Nick must have been the one to alert Wyndham. Nick was always so pious about authenticity. You could never bend him on a matter of principle.

The mask was far from being the only substitution Jorn had made. But he was very careful. He had to be. He had a lot to lose. Ted was becoming more insistent and demanding money more frequently. His drug habit was expensive, and Jorn was supporting it, however reluctantly. It was not as if Ted were actually blackmailing him. Or was it? Ted knew how much Jorn's marriage meant to him and his reluctance to give up the social façade of a wife and family, an elegant home in Greenwich. Jorn couldn't ask his wife for the money, and he had spent as much as he could of his own salary without raising suspicion. So he had no choice. He took museum objects, usually gold ones, and had them copied. Gold was easy to copy, and once Peter ran the objects through the lab tests when they were acquired, they were not likely to be retested.

Jorn was sure he could get away with it. Most museums, after all, had fakes on exhibit. It was Nick, Jorn rationalized, and his fetish of virtue and principle. Nick was out to get him, ever since he saw him in the storeroom with Ted. Jorn hadn't been fooled by Nick pretending not to know what was going on.

Jorn felt Nick's cold stare across the courtroom. If only Ted wouldn't keep dropping into my office, Jorn thought. Ted had no sense of caution. When he needed heroin, nothing on earth could calm him except the money to buy it. Jorn kept a lot of cash locked in an inner drawer of his desk for Ted when he became manic. It was quite an art balancing Ted, the curators, and his wife. In his desperate moments, and these had recently become more and more frequent, Jorn toyed with the idea of getting rid of Ted. Sometimes he was afraid that Ted would be his downfall. Then, at other times, he was sure it was Nick who was out to get him. After the curators' meeting, Jorn found himself even wondering about Samuel Wyndham. Perhaps he was on to him.

Jorn thought it was ironic. Ted was a slave to his addiction, and

Jorn was Ted's slave. With Ted he felt as if he had discovered his real self. He didn't have to pretend and be constantly on guard. Life with Elizabeth was a pretense. He appreciated her. He even loved her in some ways, and he certainly loved his children. But Jorn was afraid of Elizabeth, and he fought to keep his distance from her. He was terrified that she would destroy him each time they made love. Elizabeth attributed his aloofness to his unhappy childhood and Swedish temperament. She even teased him about it. He put up with it in good humor—anything as long as she didn't find out about the forgeries or about Ted.

Fortunately Jorn had a reliable outlet for genuine objects. That, he knew, would never be a problem. Swiss bank vaults were full of stolen art, much of it left over from Nazi confiscation of Jewish collections. The Arabs, Japanese, South Americans, and rich American and Canadian collectors were all in the market for good, expensive antiquities. Many didn't inquire about where the objects came from, and most didn't care.

"No," Jorn replied to the defense attorney's question. "I had no idea the mask was a fake. The last I heard Peter Ryan tested the metal for authenticity and the results were positive. It was a major acquisition for us and had been in the Wyndham collection for many years."

Rogers paused. Several jurors shifted in their seats.

"Now then, Mr. Hill," Rogers said, "Peter Ryan has testified that two Minoan snake goddesses had been stripped of their gold. He also testified that just before his death Samuel Wyndham ordered all the antique jewelry retested."

"That is correct."

"Looks pretty bad for your department, wouldn't you say?"

"Objection." Crawford rose. "The witness is not on trial. And neither is his department."

"Your Honor," Chris Rogers countered, "I am attempting to show the court that curators at the Wyndham Institute other than my client had motives for killing Samuel Wyndham."

"Objection overruled. You may proceed, Mr. Rogers."

Finally! thought Nick. Maybe the judge is getting the picture. Maybe he realizes how much more there is to Samuel's murder than meets the eye.

"Thank you, Your Honor." Rogers addressed Jorn. "Did you, Mr. Hill, know anything about the gold removed from the snake goddesses?"

Jorn remembered those little ivory and faïence figurines well. They had been excavated at Knossos, and he had been the one to acquire them for the Institute. He had come across them by chance at the end of the summer after digging at Santorini, the volcanic island in the Aegean Sea known as Thera in antiquity. The volcano had erupted sometime around 1400 BC and buried a flourishing civilization in ash. It hadn't been rediscovered until the 1960s when several excavations were established on the island.

That summer had been a turning point in Jorn's life. He had been married for five years when the opportunity that every archaeologist dreams of presented itself. Samuel Wyndham hired him away from his professorship and offered him his own dig at Santorini.

"I have a theory about Santorini," Wyndham confided in Jorn. "I think it is the lost Atlantis, and we know that Plato thought so as well. You're the best young scholar in the field. I want you to direct the excavation that the Wyndham Institute is sponsoring on the island."

Jorn jumped at the chance. He discussed it with Elizabeth, who encouraged him to accept. She agreed to stay at home with the children, who were just one and four, too young for the rigors of an archaeological site.

Jorn would never forget that summer. He met and fell in love with Theo, a young man from the nearby village. Each night, when work was over, Jorn would leave the site on the pretext of needing time to himself. He would meet Theo and they would make love on the beach, on the rocky shore, and among the silvery-gray olive trees. Together they would watch the sun rise from the hill tops. The white stone archway and the bell that hung inside it made a glorious silhouette against Homer's wine-dark sea. In Greece, Jorn felt that he had come home at long last. This was the land of Plato and Achilles and of the beautiful Alcibiades, who loved Socrates. If only Jorn had lived in ancient Greece, he would not have been out of step with social norms. He would not have to hide his true self. He could have Elizabeth and the boys *and* his lover. He would be thought of as normal, even virtuous.

That summer had been Jorn's first real romance. Elizabeth could never be as exciting a lover as Theo. And when he finally left Santorini, Jorn was in a state of terrible confusion. He resolved to keep his secret buried deep within him. He would never again be unfaithful to his wife. Now that he had discovered, and faced, his real self, he believed he would have the courage and strength to go on living his lie. And he had. Until last year, when Ted came to work at the Wyndham Institute.

Jorn no longer even remembered how it all began. Before he could stop himself, he was in over his head. He had to find the money Ted demanded. Now everything was closing in on him. Wyndham's death and Nick's trial, he realized, would be the way out. Jorn could kill two birds with one stone. Then he would be free. He would have Elizabeth *and* Ted.

"No, Mr. Rogers." Jorn Hill lied. "I know nothing about the disappearance of the gold snakes or any of the antique jewelry. Padrone was in charge of security at the Institute. We were in a state of chaos, you know. Anyone could have made the substitutions. The

CHAPTER 18

Friday, November 19, 4:05 p.m.

The entire mood of the courtroom eased as Frances Atwood bustled up to the witness stand. The sixty-year-old paleoanthropologist, known the world over for her work on African hominid fossils and her controversial views on evolution, was the very image of the wholesome American grandmother. She was a small, plump woman with an open, cheerful expression and eyes that smiled through the metal-framed, granny glasses attached to a chain around her neck. A mass of graying curls surrounded her face. She wore a simple, dark-brown skirt and a beige pullover decorated with a string of green jade beads. Several gold bracelets jangling noisily on her wrists contrasted with the silent step of her practical, flat, rubber-soled shoes.

Nick noticed the members of the jury relax as Frances arranged herself in the witness chair and swore to tell the truth. It felt as if a comfortable air had settled over the courtroom. He had always liked and admired Frances for her combination of honesty with enormous professional achievement. He knew that Samuel had liked her as well. But Nick couldn't help wondering what the prosecution had in store for her. Surely anything Frances said against him would have a big impact on the jury.

"I am a paleoanthropologist, a senior member of the Wyndham Institute," declared Frances matter-of-factly.

"Quite so," said Crawford. "And could you explain to the court the exact nature of your work at the Institute?"

"Certainly." Frances Atwood smiled and smoothed a wrinkle on her skirt. "I was trained in anthropology with a specialization in early hominid and hominoid fossils. I have also studied anatomy and linguistics."

"Linguistics?"

"The structure of language, young man," replied Frances sternly as if she were addressing a recalcitrant grandson who hadn't done his homework. "I am interested in human evolution, in particular the links between hominids and hominoids—or as you might say, between men and apes. I am hoping that their relationship will help us to understand the origins of civilization."

"Thank you, Dr. Atwood." Crawford had the unpleasant sensation of having been reprimanded. He turned to the jury and cleared his throat.

Nick smiled at Crawford's momentary unease. He knew that Frances often had that effect on people. The discrepancy between her genial manner and her incredible store of knowledge could be disconcerting.

Crawford was determined not to lose control of his witness. He quickly recovered his composure.

"Now then, Dr. Atwood," he said, "what can you tell the court about the argument between Nicholas d'Abernon and Samuel Wyndham after his meeting with the curators?"

"What would you like to know?" Frances asked, turning an innocent expression toward the prosecutor.

"You did overhear them, didn't you?"

"Yes, I did. But so what? Everyone has arguments. Samuel and I used to argue all the time. Doesn't mean a thing."

"That will be for the jury to decide. Please just answer the question."

"Very well then. Yes, I heard *part* of the argument."

"Was it heated?"

"Arguments with Samuel were always heated. And remember, Samuel and Nick were the best of friends. Samuel was thrilled at the prospect of Nick as a future son-in-law."

"The question, Dr. Atwood. Please confine your response to the question."

Frances gazed inquiringly at the judge, who nodded his agreement with Crawford.

"Now then, did Samuel Wyndham threaten the defendant in any way? Did he not, in fact, tell Mr. d'Abernon that he would cut him out of his will and ruin his career?"

"Well …" Frances hesitated.

Nick felt sorry for Frances Atwood. He knew she had no wish to incriminate him. She had been under a lot of strain recently herself. Nick remembered that Samuel had been worried about her, mentioned her drinking secretly in her office. Nick hadn't known Frances Atwood very long, although her worldwide reputation had made her practically a household name. Her popular book, *Watusi Women*, on the role of women in a pastoral society, had had a long run on the *New York Times* bestseller list. And it had become a staple of high school and college reading lists.

However popular that book had been, Atwood's scholarly focus laid much further back in time, in prehistory. Her interest in that subject had been stimulated in 1974, when as a first-year graduate student, she accompanied Dr. Donald Johanson to Hadar, in Ethiopia. He was leading a team investigating the local Afar culture, which dated to as far back as five million years ago. The team discovered the skull, lower jaw, and thighbone of a young adult who belonged to the early hominid species *Australopithecus afarensis*. What was remarkable about the fossil was that the thigh bone indicated that the creature was bipedal and walked upright rather than on all fours. This was one more piece of evidence of human prehistory. They named their find Lucy after the Beatles song "Lucy in the Sky with Diamonds," which they were playing as they celebrated their find. This discovery convinced Frances that human evolution extended much farther back in history than previously thought and that humans must have evolved from bipedal apes.

After she returned to school, Frances read about Raymond Dart, the controversial physician who became a paleoanthropologist, and his discovery in the dolomite cave at Makapansgat in South Africa. It was at that remote, rugged site, two hundred miles north of Johannesburg, that the African chief Makapan had marshaled three thousand of his tribesmen in a last stand against the Boers. The Boers had massacred the Africans to a man, and for years their bleached bones lay in the cave and surrounding countryside, disturbed only by the limestone workers cutting away at the face of the cave.

In coming to Makapansgat, Dart hadn't the slightest interest in recent South African history. What intrigued him was the discovery by one of the workers of a single baboon skull among the myriad of bones of the slain warriors. Before World War II, Raymond Dart had confounded the British experts on evolution with his discovery of the hominid fossil, the so-called Taung Baby. The British refused to accept Dart's identification of the fossil as an early ancestor of man, because to do so would call into question their own hominid fossil, Piltdown Man. The brain belonging to Piltdown Man was larger than the brain of the Taung Baby, and the scientific community preferred to think of man's ancestors as large-brained rather than small-brained.

Dart's views eventually prevailed, but only after Piltdown Man had been exposed—by means of the newly discovered technique of Carbon 14 dating—as a clever forgery. The hoax provoked one of the greatest scientific scandals of the twentieth century. Dart then had evidence for the unexpected existence of baboons in South Africa. This convinced him that the history of the area and its significance in terms of human evolution were far more important than previously imagined.

It was at Makapansgat that Raymond Dart made the discoveries leading to his theory that man was aggressive by nature. Frances and her future husband Roland were there when Dart found more baboon skulls—forty-two to be exact, of which twenty-seven were inexplicably smashed in on the left side. Dart theorized that the baboons had been killed by the erect, walking, right-handed hominids known as Australopithecines. He concluded that these hominids, man's ancient ancestors, killed members of a related species, ate flesh, and wielded weapons made of bone. This discovery convinced Dart that man had inherited a brutal aggressive instinct that he linked directly to modern crime and warfare. Though not without vociferous critics, Dart found champions for his views in Konrad Lorenz, Robert Ardrey, and Desmond Morris. His theory of man's innate aggressiveness was equated by some with Freud's death instinct. Frances Atwood was inspired by Dart's ideas and decided to dedicate her life to pursuing his theories. She eventually became one of the leading scholars in the field. Several years later, inspired by the discoveries of Dart and Johanson, Atwood led her own expedition to Makapansgat.

It was during this trip that Frances met her husband, the dashing, dynamic Australian geologist who was part of the excavation team. Roland Atwood was tall and graceful with a mass of wavy brown hair. He was charming, intelligent, and to Frances intensely romantic. His biography as a geological explorer read like an adventure story. By the time Roland met Frances, he had located precious and semiprecious ore in unlikely places all over the world: emeralds in the Amazon, gold in the Arizona mountains, and sapphires in India. He had published three books on his adventures, all of which combined sound scholarship with popular appeal. Roland joined Frances's expedition to South Africa for two reasons: he was genuinely interested in contributing to studies of evolution, and at the same time, the rogue in him hoped to make lucrative contacts with South African diamond miners.

Nick wondered what Wyndham could have discovered about Frances that was making her drink so heavily. It seemed completely out of character. Her husband, Nick knew, had died tragically when he fell into one of the many dolomite caves that honeycombed the South African landscape. But that had been years ago. Surely Frances wouldn't still be affected by his death. And as far as Nick could tell, she had no other cause for depression. She was famous, respected, and at the summit of a remarkable career.

Why, Nick wondered, should she suddenly begin drinking? Maybe Samuel had been mistaken, although Nick had to admit that she seemed a bit harried lately since collaborating with Stanley Braithwaite on her biography. And there had been that time when Nick had nearly walked right into Braithwaite one evening as he was leaving the Institute.

"Excuse me," Nick had said.

"Think nothing of it," Braithwaite replied. "But I would be grateful if you would check on Dr. Atwood. She seems rather down at the moment. We have been discussing her husband's death. Tragic, very tragic. I think it haunts her even now."

"Sure, be glad to." And Nick had gone to Frances's office. He was puzzled when she did not reply to his knock. He knew she was in. He knocked again and then tried the door. It was locked.

"Frances!" Nick called softly at first. And then louder. "What's going on? Are you all right?" Then he heard a crash. It sounded, he realized later, like a glass shattering. "Frances!" he called again.

"I hear you," she said finally. Her voice was unmistakably fuzzy.

"What's going on?" Nick repeated. "Is everything okay?"

"Yes, Nick, I'm fine. Nothing to worry about. I dropped a box of skull fragments. You go on home. It's getting late. I'll see you tomorrow."

"Well, are you sure?" Nick sensed that Frances did not want to be disturbed.

"Yes, I'm sure. Good night, Nick."

"Good night, Frances."

Nick realized that she hadn't told the truth about the skull fragments, but he decided not to interfere for the moment. Still, it was odd. The incident was so unlike Frances. Nick had never known her to lock her door.

"Yes, Dr. Atwood?" Crawford prompted.

"They did argue after the meeting," Frances conceded. "And Samuel did threaten Nick, but—"

"His exact words, please, Dr. Atwood."

"Oh, very well," she snapped. "Sam told Nick he would not allow him to take charge of the Wyndham Institute and that he would use his influence to prevent his employment elsewhere. But I know that's nonsense. Samuel got that way sometimes. He always had to be right. Nick was one of the few people who had the self-confidence to stand up to him."

"Thank you, Dr. Atwood. That will be all." Crawford sat down.

Chris Rogers rose to cross-examine.

Frances visibly relaxed and looked at him expectantly.

"Dr. Atwood," Rogers began, "you stated that you and Samuel Wyndham often argued. Could you tell the court about that?"

"Certainly." Frances rearranged herself in the witness chair. "Sam was an old tyrant. Wouldn't hear of anyone questioning his judgment. He only listened to me—once in a while, that is, and only because we were old friends. And because we were closer in age than he was to the younger curators. I tried to convince him that he could not assume his entire staff was trustworthy. You never know about people. I particularly objected to him giving every curator coded keys and access to the security system. Joe Padrone told him the same thing. It all had to do with our ideas about human nature, you see."

"Could you explain to the jury what you mean?" Rogers asked.

"Well, it's a question of evolution, really. I have seen those smashed skulls in Africa with my own eyes. We have a few of them right here at the Institute. I know very well that man inherited a killer instinct from his distant ancestors. Millions of years ago, that is. Call it what you will, aggression, the death instinct. I call it the Neanderthal Factor." Frances paused and then explained.

"When we are fetuses, we go through all the stages of evolution. And each stage leaves a trace in our brains. In my opinion, the Neanderthal Factor is responsible for our tribal instincts and inability to cooperate in forming stable societies. I am convinced that these characteristics lie at the root of human violence and aggression. Each and every one of us has a little bit of Neanderthal Man buried in our unconscious minds."

"Really, Your Honor, I must object," Crawford rose wearily. "What on earth can this possibly have to do with Samuel Wyndham's murder?"

The judge turned to Chris Rogers.

"I assure you, Your Honor," Rogers said, "that this is very relevant to my client's defense. The Wyndham Institute was not only the setting for Wyndham's murder; it was also rife with conflict."

"Very well, then. Let's get on with it. Objection overruled."

"Thank you, Your Honor." Rogers resumed.

"Please continue, Dr. Atwood."

"All right, young man. Sam had a very different view than I did. Even though he had discovered *Homo jekyllensis* himself, and even though he was acutely aware of man's potential destructive influences, he was convinced that the forces of civilization were capable of keeping them in check. In his view, the advances made by *Homo sapiens* made it possible for us to overcome and control our aggressive instincts. He had to believe that, you see, because of his breakdown."

"Breakdown?" Rogers inquired.

"Yes, after serving in Vietnam. It was as a result of his breakdown that he decided to dedicate his life to peace and culture. He was convinced that the arts and the intellectual achievements of man were the only hope for the future of civilization. Without this conviction, his life's work and the Institute would be meaningless. If his curators—and he thought of them as *his*—who were chosen, as they were, from the elite of their respective fields, couldn't be trusted, then who could? We used to argue about that a lot. I often challenged him and tried to tell him it was dangerous to put too much faith in human beings."

Frances Atwood knew from her own experience about the so-called Neanderthal Factor lying in wait beneath the surface of civilized man. She would never forget that even her own façade, her fame, her position would crumble at any moment if the truth about her was ever exposed.

From the day she met Roland Atwood she was trapped. He was like a drug, dangerously intoxicating. She had always been physically plain and unsure of herself with men. Her father used to tell her she was lucky to have brains because God gave the beauty to her older sister. "You and I got the brains," he would say. "Your mother's good looks went to Jennifer." And Jennifer had become a model and an actress. Frances became a scholar. Jennifer had all the dates in school. Even her rejected suitors didn't hang around to try for Frances.

At first Frances didn't understand why Roland married *her* of all the women available to him. He could have had his choice of anyone. She couldn't believe her good fortune when, in the middle of the South African bush, Roland proposed. True, they had been working together, making significant and exciting discoveries by correlating the geological strata with the dates of the fossils. And true, the closeness that developed on an expedition of that kind, far removed from civilized society, was unusually intense. But Roland had been in similar situations before.

Frances was so swept away by Roland that she dismissed any doubts she might have had. She accepted his proposal, and the world seized on the marriage as a fabulous romantic saga. The press never tired of stories about the dashing geologist and his famous wife. Roland and Frances became celebrities on four continents. The African backdrop of their lives turned their existence into a journalist's dream with jungle, bush, and veldt. Over that exotic scene was superimposed the filter of sophisticated Europe and America. But behind the glitter, in the privacy of their lives together, lay the sordid truth.

"I can't help it, Frances," Roland had told her when she confronted him. "I need variety, don't you see? I can't ask someone like you to play my games."

At first Frances did not understand. As time went on, she realized that he was compelled to act out fantasies of domination and submission with other women. She was overwhelmed with conflicting emotions of jealousy and disgust. She didn't know what to do. Just as Roland needed the women and the satisfaction of his fantasies, Frances needed Roland.

Some nights Roland didn't come back at all. Occasionally Frances found herself locked out of their hotel bedroom. She had to wait downstairs in the lounge, pretending she wanted a nightcap. Alcohol became her crutch. But whenever she had a drink, frightening thoughts entered her head, thoughts of murder and revenge. Sometimes she felt as though Roland were an addiction from which she would never be free. If he were simply not there, she rationalized, then the temptation would be gone forever. She would be free of her chains. Such thoughts continually preoccupied her even when she was sober, until eventually they consumed her completely. And when it happened, it seemed so easy, so natural.

It happened on a return trip to Makapansgat. They were exploring among the caves when Frances heard the sound of falling rocks. Then she heard Roland.

"Frances!" Roland screamed. "Help me!"

Frances did it without thinking. She stepped hard on Roland's grasping fingers as he tried to hold on to the ledge. He screamed again and fell. Frances heard the crash and the echo from deep within the cave. And then there was silence, ominous silence, liberating silence in the great expanse of the African landscape. She was alone and she was finally free. She knew that his body would never be found. The authorities suspected nothing, nor did anyone else. Roland Atwood's death was billed in the press as a romantic tragedy.

Later Frances realized that both she and Roland had been enslaved by the destructive side of their characters. In her more cynical moments, she put it down to the Neanderthal Factor in both of them.

"Might one infer, Dr. Atwood, that Samuel Wyndham unwittingly put himself in danger by trusting his staff?"

"Yes, of course."

"Objection!" Crawford was on his feet. "That is an inference, not a fact."

"Sustained."

Nick was dejected and felt his situation was hopeless. It was one thing to suggest that other curators had motives to kill Samuel, but none of them seemed to have had the opportunity—that is, if Montoya's testimony were to be believed. And Nick knew it wasn't. Someone else had been in Wyndham's office, and that person was the murderer. But how could he prove it? Nick had the distinct impression that Rogers was spinning his wheels. His line of questioning was going nowhere. He glanced at Frances, who smiled encouragingly at him. Nick felt better.

"Dr. Atwood," Rogers began again. "You say that you and Samuel Wyndham were friends, and yet you often argued with him. Was he likely to have heated arguments with anyone he disagreed with?"

Frances knew that Samuel was not only her friend, but also that he had covered up for her. Ever since that biographer had been at the Institute interviewing her about her past, she had begun to fall apart, especially as he focused on her marriage. She had thought it was all behind her, but she found it difficult to maintain the romantic image of her life with Roland in the face of Braithwaite's insistent questioning. And lately, she had been plagued with nightmares. She dreamed of Roland falling through dark caverns and saw herself running across the African veldt pursued by ominous clouds. In the worst nightmares, hordes of baboons chased her with clubs as she ran in place, unable to escape. She would awake screaming until she realized it was a dream.

In order to avoid the nightmares, Frances forced herself to stay awake. She worked late and calmed her fraying nerves with Johnny Walker. Sam knew something was wrong. He came upon her one evening when she was so drunk she didn't realize what she was saying. "It was murder, Sam," she admitted. "Never forget the Neanderthal Factor in all of us," she warned him. "It always finds a way." Sam had tried to calm her, pretending to ignore her confession. She knew he must have known the truth. Yet he never referred to it. He suggested that she take a rest, a vacation. Frances was grateful to Sam, except when the drinking started. After several glasses of Scotch she would begin to worry that he might contact the police. Was he really as loyal as he seemed? she wondered. Or was he pretending, leading her into a false sense of security until the day he would openly reveal her terrible and hidden crime?

And what about Nick? How much did he suspect? Had he and Sam discussed her drinking? Sometimes Sam and Nick got mixed up in her mind, and Frances would black out in the confusion. The trial, dreadful as Frances knew it must be for Nick and Ruth, was a blessing for her. It gave her a respite from Braithwaite's questions. She told him they would not meet as long as the trial was in session and the Institute in an uproar over Samuel's murder. With the intolerable weight of that pressure lifted, Frances was her old self again.

"Yes, young man," Frances assured Rogers. "Sam was a great one for an argument. It's just coincidence that he fought with Nick before he was killed. Unfortunately, Sam's beloved Institute is a nest of vipers, and a lot of people were threatened by his realization that corruption was rampant."

"Objection!" roared Crawford.

"Sustained. Strike that last remark from the record," ordered the judge.

"No further questions. Thank you, Dr. Atwood."

Nick breathed a sigh of relief. There it was, out in the open once again. Even though Crawford's objection had been sustained,

CHAPTER 19

Friday, November 19, 5:05 p.m.

Frances Atwood was the last witness for the prosecution. After she had completed her testimony, Sinclair Crawford rested his case. He hadn't ended on the note he had wished, but he was satisfied with the evidence against Nick d'Abernon. And he had to admit that the publicity surrounding the trial might work to his political advantage. His name had been on the front page every day for the past week. Crawford was also pleased that his side of the case finished up on a Friday and that the judge had ordered the court to reconvene the following Wednesday in order to give the defense two additional days to prepare its case. That would give him a long, relaxing weekend with his family. He thought he might drive up to Vermont for a couple of days of skiing.

Crawford didn't envy Rogers. He could easily imagine the care with which the defense lawyer would sift through every scrap of material in the hope of finding some overlooked piece of evidence in his client's favor. But unless he had a miracle up his sleeve, and Crawford sincerely doubted he did, things looked pretty bleak for d'Abernon. Crawford collected his papers, put them in his Mark

Cross briefcase, and started out of the courtroom. He noticed that d'Abernon and Rogers were still at the defense table deep in conversation.

"We had better do some serious thinking over the next few days, Nick," Rogers said with an unmistakable air of concern in his voice. "I want you to go over everything, every detail. Maybe something will occur to you. It's a long shot, but it's all we've got. We have to discredit Montoya and show that someone besides you was in your office the night of the murder."

Nick nodded but didn't answer. There wasn't much to say. He did not look forward to spending the weekend cooped up in a dreary jail cell.

"Listen, Chris," Nick finally said, "I want you to make sure that Ruth can visit me this afternoon. I've got to explain to her what happened with Lillian."

"For God's sake, Nick. Will you keep your mind on the trial?! There won't be any Ruth if you are convicted. Oh, all right," Rogers sighed. "I'll catch up with her now. She's waiting for me outside."

Ruth searched for Padrone as she left the courtroom. If ever she felt the need for his warm, protective presence, it was now. She didn't spot him in the crowd slowly filing through the heavy wooden doors, but she was sure he would be outside. She allowed herself to be pushed along into the corridor. Ahead of her she saw Lillian Nakamura rushing away. Lillian seemed determined to escape the crowd of reporters. As Ruth watched the retreating figure, she felt betrayed. What is the matter with Nick? she thought. He had better have a good reason for not telling me about Lillian. And to have it all come out in court and end up in the media.

"Ruth!" The sound of her name jolted her from her train of thought. She whirled around and confronted Roger's narrow, worried face. He was, she noticed, barely as tall as she. "Ruth," he said, "Nick is anxious to see you."

"Is he, Chris?" Ruth noticed Ricardo edging his way through the crowd toward her. He had a slightly amused, yet quizzical, expression. "Excuse me, Chris," Ruth said. "Please tell Nick I can't see him now."

Ruth made up her mind. Angry as she was with Nick for hiding his affair with Lillian, she knew he was innocent and could never have murdered her father. If Lillian's testimony had upset her so much, she could imagine the damaging effect it would have on the jury. If anything was to be done, Ruth realized, she would have to be the one to do it. She would start with Ricardo. She was certain that Ricardo had lied when he testified that no one but her father entered Nick's office. Someone else must have been there, and she was determined to find out who it was.

Ruth waited until Ricardo was at her side. "If your invitation still stands," she said, "I would be delighted to have dinner with you tomorrow night."

Ricardo smiled. "What an unexpected pleasure. I'll pick you up at eight."

Rogers shrugged.

Jorn Hill had become separated from his wife as he left the courtroom. She had stayed behind chatting with Frances Atwood and the crowd had come between them. Jorn decided to wait by the door, knowing that Elizabeth would surely notice his towering figure. He was close to panic. He suspected that everyone knew what he had done, or if they didn't now, they soon would. Wyndham's death hadn't changed a thing. He had to think of some other way. But he was overwhelmed and nearly paralyzed by a sudden feeling of total helplessness. He froze as he felt the familiar hand of Ted Curtis on the small of his back.

"For God's sake, Ted!" Jorn whispered. "This is not the place."

"Why the hell didn't you come to the Institute as I asked? I waited for you all afternoon. That was a fucking rotten thing to do. I'm strung out. Ricardo won't give me any more until you pay him. And I can't last much longer."

Jorn saw the beads of perspiration on Ted's forehead. He recognized the glazed eyes, the imploring yet menacing look. He felt Ted's hand tremble against his backbone. He *was* strung out; Jorn knew it only too well. And that was dangerous.

"I couldn't come, you fool. I had to be in court. Go on back to the Institute right now. Wait in my office. I'll be there as soon as I can. I'll take care of Ricardo. Go now! Elizabeth is coming." Jorn twisted himself away from Ted's grasp. He tried to summon up a smile as he waved to his wife.

"You'd better show up this time," whispered Ted behind him. He darted away as Elizabeth approached.

"Who was that nervous man you were talking to, darling? Haven't I seen him at the Institute?"

"P-probably," Jorn stammered, frantically searching for a pretext to get back there. He found one and replied as calmly as he could. "That's Ted, he's in charge of lighting. He's having some technical problems with one of the exhibitions and wants my advice. I agreed to help him. If you don't mind, Elizabeth," Jorn strained to sound casual. "I'll go back to the Institute. You take the car home and I'll catch a train later. I'll call to let you know which one."

"I could come to the Institute and wait for you there."

"No, not this time; I don't know how long it will take."

Charles Dudley was one of the last to leave the courtroom. He had nowhere in particular to go, and he wasn't in any hurry to get home. Perhaps, he thought, there is still time to invite guests around for drinks or dinner. At least that way he could avoid the inevitable game of one-upmanship with Margaret. Better still, he'd go to his club, have a couple of stiff gins, and pick up a few rounds of backgammon. To hell with Margaret! Just as he made up his mind, Dudley saw his wife elbowing her way through the crowded courtroom toward him. She was swathed in sable. The collar of her coat was turned up to meet the brim of her sable hat, which was covered with a fine layer of powdery snow. She must have just come in from outside, thought Dudley, and it must still be freezing. He wondered what could have enticed her out of the house in such weather, certainly not the trial. Whatever it was, he knew it couldn't be good.

"Darling," Margaret called, beaming a smile across the hallway. She caught up to him. "I thought you'd like to know that we have a visitor at home, an old friend of yours from those unforgettable golden days of your youth at Cambridge."

Dudley's heart sank. Panic set in. The moment Margaret was beside him, her public smile disappeared and an entirely unfamiliar expression came over her face. It was a combination of surprise and, was it possible, grudging admiration.

"Dear Nigel told me all about his last letter, darling. Perhaps I have misjudged you."

"What is that supposed to mean?" Dudley was on guard.

"Perhaps you do have balls, after all, my dear."

When Sinclair Crawford returned to his office, he cleared his desk for the weekend. His phone rang.

"The mayor wants an update."

"It's an open-and-shut case. Rogers has nothing. By next week it will be over."

CHAPTER 20

Friday, November 19, 7:00 p.m.

Nadim's cell phone rang. He flipped it open.

"There's a new development." The monotone of the voice told Nadim that the phone was equipped with a device that disguised the identity of the speaker. Nevertheless, he knew who it had to be. He generally received his orders from Cairo in coded hieroglyphs. This was only the second time that a directive was coming from higher up, from the leader of the cell. The voice had been disguised exactly the same way the first time. It must be serious.

"We have an additional mandate. They have decided to renew the offensive and target cultural sites. The first target is the Wyndham Institute. You know what you have to do."

The speaker was pleased that things were falling into place and revenge would not be long in coming. Wyndham was dead, d'Abernon was out of the picture, and soon the Institute would be history. But one loose end still had to be tied up.

Being recruited by Al-Qaeda had been a stroke of luck, because while the speaker would be useful to them, they had provided the speaker with the means and opportunity to pursue a different agenda.

CHAPTER 21

Saturday, November 20, 8:10 p.m.

Ricardo Montoya turned up the collar of his overcoat as he rounded the corner of Lexington Avenue and Eighty-First Street and met an icy blast of wind. He stopped at a newsstand, his attention caught by the evening headline:

FAMOUS ANTRHOPOLOGIST CITES "NEANDERTHAL FACTOR" IN WYNDHAM MURDER TRIAL

Silly old bitch! Montoya was not pleased. *Thank God Frances doesn't really know what happened that night.* Montoya continued on, bracing himself against the cold. *The so-called Neanderthal Factor wasn't going to do d'Abernon much good, judging from the testimony so far. And that was just fine with him.* Ricardo's mind went back over the previous afternoon. *What a wonderful surprise Lillian's testimony had been! Ricardo hadn't thought d'Abernon, Mr. Rectitude and Principle himself, had it in him. And neither had Ruth, judging from her expression. Not to mention her decision to have dinner with him while her boyfriend sat in jail. Maybe Ruth* was finally seeing the light. She had far too much to offer to waste it on d'Abernon. Tonight Ricardo would show Ruth what life in New York with *him* could be like.

Ricardo arrived at Ruth's door. He hadn't expected the house to be quite so grand. But then he knew Ruth had recently moved, and she was, after all, a Wyndham. In the past year, her career had taken off. She had been discovered by Paris and Milan, and her dress designs were now a permanent fixture in *Vogue, Elle,* and *La Moda.* Ricardo rang the bell and waited. No answer. He checked his watch: 8:12 p.m. He inspected the bell for names. There were two bells. The name R. Wyndham was above the smaller bell at the top. Below, by the larger bell, he saw a brass plate engraved with WYNDHAM DESIGNS. Thinking that Ruth might have lost track of the time, he decided to try that one. Almost immediately the door opened, and a strikingly attractive, tall, and very thin young woman smiled at him.

"Mr. Montoya, please come in. Ruth is expecting you. She had some last minute things to do in the showroom. You can meet her there, if you like, or if you prefer, you can wait upstairs. I am Marianna, by the way."

"I'll follow you. It would be a privilege to see the latest Wyndham designs."

Marianna led Ricardo through the oval entrance hall, across the black-and-white marble floor. The walls were painted a pale salmon color, which set off the white, fluted Ionic pilasters. Marianna opened tall mahogany doors at the end of the hallway and Ricardo found himself in a spacious rectangular room. Opposite the entrance were two double French windows looking out onto an enchanting, snow-covered garden. It was illuminated by tiny white lights strung along the branches of a large tree at the center of circular patterns of slate tiles.

The room itself was formal, but at the same time it felt warm and comfortable. Two matching sofas were arranged on either side of a Corralito marble fireplace with an exquisitely carved Rococo mantel. Eighteenth century. Ricardo recognized the style as that of Grindling Gibbons. Like the curtains framing the French windows, the sofas were covered in a dusky-rose velvet. Several smaller sofas and groups of chairs were organized to form additional seating arrangements. They were set off by the soft beige of the walls and the carved white moldings. An Aubusson carpet picked up the colors of the upholstery and the walls and added highlights of blue. On a marble-topped table opposite the fireplace stood an enormous cobalt-blue glass vase filled with dozens of pink-flecked white lilies. The reflection of the delicate, sculptured flowers filled the smoky surface of the mirror above the mantel.

Ricardo appreciated the taste and style of the room. He noticed that Ruth was standing by a rack of dresses discretely located in the corner behind a screen. She was replacing one of her designs.

"May I see it?" Ricardo asked.

Ruth spun around. "Of course. Marianna will take your coat."

Ricardo handed over his coat.

Ruth held up the dress. It was an exquisitely cut, long black sheath. The stem of a single lotus flower seemed to grow from the scalloped hemline and was appliquéd to the bodice. The simplicity of the cut, together with the natural appearance of the flower, produced a stunning effect that Ricardo appreciated as much as the décor.

"It's magnificent, Ruth, really magnificent. I am truly impressed."

"Thank you, Ricardo. Shall we go upstairs and have a drink? You haven't seen that part of the house yet."

Ruth hung the dress on the rack. She wore Turkish harem pants, whose voluminous folds were a deep, shimmering purple silk. They were severely tapered around her slender ankles. The high, wide waist emphasized her tall, graceful figure. Her white crepe de chine blouse had enormous sleeves and wide French cuffs. The only jewelry Ruth wore was a pair of gold hoop earrings. She didn't wear, and didn't need to wear, makeup.

Ruth took Ricardo's hand and led him back through the entrance hall and up the curving staircase. From the landing Ricardo had a clear view of the entire first floor. To the left he could see into the living room and the large windows looking out onto the street below. To the right was a formal dining room overlooking the garden. Both rooms were separated from the landing by archways, and the landing itself was lined with bookshelves.

The Steinway grand piano Ruth inherited from her mother dominated the space. It was covered with photographs of members of the Wyndham family in antique silver frames. This was a much cozier room than the one downstairs. It was obvious that Ruth liked to relax here, with an old sofa and two wing chairs drawn around the fireplace. A log fire was burning behind a brass screen. The coffee table was piled high with books, magazines, and newspapers. Additional bookshelves lined the far side of the room, together with a computer, printer, Bose radio and CD player. As a final touch that appealed to Ricardo, the room was filled with plants and bowls of bulbs—daffodils, tulips, and amaryllis—in different stages of growth. The delicate, sweet aroma of freesias permeated the air from a vase on the sideboard.

"What will you drink, Ricardo? I know how much you like sherry, and I have a Manzanilla Pasada from Hidalgo that I think you will enjoy."

Riccardo took the bottle Ruth offered him and with a twist removed the cork. He poured the sherry into two sherry glasses, deftly twisting the bottle to avoid spilling even a drop.

He raised his glass to Ruth. "To new beginnings. This is a fabulous place, and your taste is perfect."

They sat by the fire for a while, chatting amicably and carefully avoiding any reference to Nick's trial.

"It's almost too comfortable to leave here," said Ricardo. "And the sherry is delicious. But you have an important decision to make, Ruth."

"And what might that be?" Ruth smiled as she sipped her sherry.

"Well, I didn't know what your mood would be tonight, so I made three different dinner reservations. You have a choice of gloom, glitter, or grandeur."

Ruth laughed. "Glitter," she said. "Definitely glitter. It's time for some glitter in my life."

"Glitter it shall be. And one more thing."

"Yes?"

"Can we agree that tonight is just for us?"

"I'd love it, Ricardo." Ruth sensed that the last thing he wanted to talk about was the trial. She'd have to find a way to work up to the subject if she were going to achieve her ends. Perhaps over dinner ...

The restaurant was one of the current "in" places in Tribeca. It was elegant, French, crowded, and very expensive. It had dark paneled walls, a plush plum-colored carpet, dimly lit brass chandeliers, and intricately etched and frosted glass windows. On each of the tables, with starched white tablecloths and huge napkins folded in the shape of cones, stood a sterling silver vase with a single red rose.

"*Bonsoir, Monsieur Montoya,*" boomed the maître d' as Ricardo and Ruth came in from the cold. He ushered them past the curved, art nouveau bar toward the dining room. "*Un plaisir, comme toujours. Suivez-moi, s'il vous plait.*"

He led the couple to a corner table protected from the din of the crowd.

"*Merci, Henri.*"

Ruth noticed Ricardo slip him a folded bill.

"*De rien,*" the maître d' replied with a smile and a bow. "*Bon appetit.*"

Just as Ruth settled in to her seat, one of the waiters, an old pro in shirt sleeves, a black bow tie, and a long white apron, arrived with a bottle of Dom Perignon. He showed the label to Ricardo, who nodded approvingly. Then he opened it and filled two long-stemmed, crystal champagne glasses. A second waiter followed on his heels bearing two plates of Belon oysters arranged on beds of crushed ice.

"Ricardo, what a surprise! I don't even have to think about what to order. Everything just arrives. Am I to be entirely in your capable hands tonight?"

"Nothing would please me more. Remember, tonight is dedicated to you and to us. What I want to hear about is how you are. We haven't spoken together for so long that I've lost track of what you've been up to. But when I go to parties, I always recognize the Wyndham designs draped on New York's most fashionable shoulders. I want you to tell me how it feels to be known for what you have accomplished and not simply because your last name happens to be Wyndham."

Ricardo could be charming when he wanted to, which was often, and especially when it was useful. He had an unfailing knack for drawing people out, a knack that he both enjoyed and cultivated. He could learn a great deal that way. But in Ruth's case he was genuinely interested. Samuel Wyndham's daughter had intrigued him from their first meeting. He thought she was without guile and completely uncalculating. At first he refused to believe it was possible. He did not meet many people without some kind of agenda.

Although Ruth was clever and by no means unworldly, she had a fresh innocence and enthusiasm that made her different from the old-world cynicism in which he had grown up. Ruth seemed to be only herself. She weighed things carefully and refused to be swayed by fashion or fads. In short, Ruth was unlike any other woman Ricardo had ever known. He realized that he was half in love with her and wondered if his infatuation were simply the result of her slightly distant air. She was one of a very few women who had not instantly fallen at his feet. It fact, it was quite obvious that after Nick appeared on the scene, Ruth was off limits. This galled Ricardo to no end. He intended to devote tonight to changing that. The challenge of it excited him. Perhaps that was all there was to it. But he couldn't be sure.

Ricardo had hit on just the thing that Ruth was most proud of. She was glad she had finally made Wyndham her own name as well as her father's. The thought of her father saddened her. He would not be able to share in her success, and Ruth knew he would have enjoyed it. She could never tell him how much she owed him or how grateful she was for his encouragement to be independent and self-reliant.

Ruth felt Ricardo's hand close over hers and knew he had sensed her thoughts correctly. She looked up and met his dark eyes gazing intently into her own.

"He was a great man, Ruth. Difficult, overbearing at times, but he had grand vision and even greater courage in following it. I think you take after him."

Now's my chance, thought Ruth. She grew serious. "Yes, he was a great man. I haven't told anyone yet, but he wrote me a long letter just before he died. Joe Padrone showed it to me yesterday. He found it pushed in back of some books in father's office."

Ruth noticed the momentary flicker of interest in Ricardo's eyes, which he quickly concealed. She continued, trying to calculate exactly how much to reveal. "Father had some pretty disturbing things to say about the Institute, Ricardo. He wrote me because he knew someone might try to kill him. He wanted me to know as much as he did, just in case. And I guess he also wanted to document what he had found out."

"And what was that, Ruth?" The edge to Ricardo's voice was unmistakable.

Ruth wasn't at all sure how to proceed. She knew that Ricardo was too smart to be trapped easily into incriminating himself. But he *was* vain. And his disdain for the other curators at the Institute was no secret. Unless *he* had been the one to remove the pages from her father's letter, he wouldn't know that she was bluffing. She decided it was worth the risk.

"He thought Jorn was responsible for at least one of the forgeries," Ruth said, pretending as if she were revealing a major secret, when in fact, the only thing she had to go on was what had been revealed during the trial and not anything her father had written on the missing pages. "And he knew that Lillian was faking provenances."

"Oh, is that all?" Ricardo laughed. His relief was obvious. "Don't look so shocked, my dear. We all knew about the little scams of Jorn and Lillian. It's par for the course in the museum world. I'm sure the fashion business has its own arrangements as well."

"But Ricardo ..."

Before Ruth could continue the waiter arrived with the main course. Ricardo had ordered a classic French duck *à l'orange* with wild rice and a Chateau Latour Pauillac.

Ruth hadn't realized how hungry she was, and she enjoyed every mouthful of the duck with its caramel glaze, thin slices of orange, and grated orange rind. She realized that the conversation about the Wyndham Institute was over for the moment. She would try again later.

During dinner Ricardo became his charming self again. Ruth enjoyed his questions and was happy to describe the ups and downs of the fashion world. It was an unpredictable business and sometimes amusing.

"The worst moment of all," she said, referring to her fall show, "happened when a scrawny alley cat scampered into the showroom through one of the open French windows. Close on its heels came an enormous and very determined tomcat."

"Sounds like a Latin lover to me."

"I hope Latin lovers are a bit more discreet," Ruth replied. "The scene on my Aubusson carpet caused quite a stir. My best model broke into gales of laughter, and so did everyone else. Fortunately I managed to throw a blanket over the cats and remove them before the situation got completely out of hand." Ricardo laughed.

"Ruth, will you come home with me for a night cap? I bet you don't know how to make a pousse-café."

"A what?" Ruth had no idea what Ricardo was talking about, but she seized the excuse to prolong the evening and pump him for information. "I have no idea what you are talking about," she said, "but I would love to find out."

CHAPTER 22

Saturday, November 20, 8:45 p.m.

Joe Padrone grumbled to himself as he trudged up the steps of Riker's Island House of Detention. A light snow had begun to fall and the streets were slippery. He checked his watch: 8:45 p.m. Padrone was annoyed. This was not his idea of how to spend a cold Saturday night. Getting to Riker's Island was extremely inconvenient. Padrone had taken the bus over the Fifty-Ninth Street Bridge to Queens and from there to Riker's Island, where he had to wait while his pass was approved. Then he had to wait for a second bus to the Detention building. He could think of about a thousand things he'd rather be doing.

When the trial was adjourned until the following Wednesday, Nick returned to his cell, while Padrone consoled himself with a good Italian meal. Now, only because of his promise to Ruth, he was going to make one last attempt to talk to Nick. Joe clapped his hands together to warm them up. He was not looking forward to this meeting. As far as he was concerned, there was no doubt about Nick's guilt, with or without Samuel's letter. The guy was caught red-handed. Padrone had never much liked Nick, anyway. And

Lillian's testimony was the last straw. He felt terribly sorry for Ruth and furious at Nick. Not that the rest of the Wyndham staff was any better. Padrone realized that they were all up to no good. So much for so-called intellectuals, he told himself. But he was determined to help Ruth see that Nick was the wrong choice for her.

Padrone banged on the old door to the Men's House of Detention. He stomped his feet and shook the snow off his shoes. Finally, a guard opened up. He knew Padrone. "Coming to see the famous killer, Joe? Quite a celebrity you got yourself this time. Doesn't look good for him about now. What's all the press about a Neanderthal lady?"

Padrone grinned. "I need to see him, Jimmy. Can you arrange it?"

"It's kinda late." The guard glanced at the wall clock. "I guess it's okay. We'll say it's in connection with the trial. So go on in. I'll call ahead for you."

"Thanks, pal, I owe you one."

Because of all the publicity surrounding his trial, Nick was not with the other prisoners held without bail pending their trials. He was under administrative segregation in a separate wing. Since his trial was in progress, he was allowed to receive visitors at any time except during the designated hours reserved for sleeping.

Padrone went through the usual entry ritual of signing in, showing his ID card and submitting to the metal detector. He trudged down the long, dreary corridor, its buff-colored, peeling walls illuminated by fluorescent lights. The barred door leading to the visitors' room clanged as a guard opened it and motioned Joe to a chair inside. Except for two plain wooden chairs, a table, and a single ceiling light, the room was empty. Padrone sat down.

He didn't have to wait long for the guards to arrive with Nick, who looked drained and pale. He was in the orange jail uniform that prisoners were required to wear when meeting with visitors. It was supposed to minimize security risks.

"I'll never get used to this outfit," said Nick as he glanced down at the trousers. "What brings you here on a night like this?" Nick sat down opposite Padrone. "Ruth refused to come."

"If it weren't for her, d'Abernon, believe me, I wouldn't be here either. After what she heard in court today, I can understand why she's not here. It's beyond me why she ever gave you the time of day anyway."

Nick knew Padrone meant Lillian's testimony. "Listen, Joe, that's old history. It has nothing to do with Ruth and me now."

"Lillian doesn't seem to think so," Padrone snapped back.

"Okay, Joe, out with it. Surely you didn't come all the way over here to discuss an ancient romance. It happened long before I met Ruth. Besides, you must know I was framed. You've had your own problems in the past."

"Right, buddy." Padrone knew Nick was referring to his own departure from the NYPD under a cloud of suspicion, and he did not appreciate the reference. Nor did he appreciate the fact that Nick knew about it. "This is my last visit." Joe got up and paced angrily around the room. "Let's hear what you've got to say for yourself. As far as I'm concerned, you're guilty of murder one."

Nick felt fury well up in him. He watched Padrone circle the room like a wild animal stalking his prey. Nick was the prey. "You've had it in for me ever since I came to the Institute. Don't think I don't know why. It's Ruth, isn't it? You don't think I'm good enough for her."

Padrone stifled an impulse to grab Nick and throttle him. He controlled himself with difficulty. "Remember me?" he said in a biting, sarcastic tone. "I'm the guy who walked into your office one night and just happened to see you standing over Samuel's dead body with the murder weapon in your hands."

"I didn't do it."

"Prove it! Go ahead, convince me."

"I don't have to. They have to prove I did it."

Padrone shook his head in disbelief. "You really are something, d'Abernon. You were caught practically in the act, with the blood still fresh and dripping from the ax, the works. Even got your fingerprints."

"Of course you got my fingerprints, you asshole! It's *my* office we're talking about, remember?" Nick pounded the table.

"What about the ax?" Padrone persisted.

"I was using it for research," Nick replied between clenched teeth.

"And the blood? Were you using that for research too?"

"I should never have picked up the ax."

"And the argument? I suppose that was a tea party? You know, I never did like your type. Research indeed. Ridiculous. You think just because I'm a cop, you intellectual snobs can lord it over me!"

Nick jumped up and glared at Padrone. "*Were* a cop, Padrone. Didn't they run you out of the force for stealing, or covering up, or something?" Nick felt the blood pounding in his head.

"You fucking bastard! I've had just about enough of you. First you seduce Ruth, then you kill her father. And for what? Money? Prestige? Hah! Look where it got you. You hypocrite." Padrone was so mad he could barely speak.

Nick's rage, compounded by fatigue and Padrone's accusations, finally got control of him and broke his resolve. "Okay, Padrone. You're going to hear it. Your great hero, Samuel Peale Wyndham, right? Well, brace yourself. He was a liar, a fake and a cheat. Your precious, God-like Wyndham falsified evidence. How about that, Padrone?" Nick sat down and looked defeated. He'd finally said it.

Padrone was taken aback. This was not at all what he had expected. "And what is that supposed to mean?" he asked suspiciously. This was a new angle for which Padrone was totally unprepared. He suddenly had the feeling that something was going on that he knew nothing about. "I think you'd better explain yourself, d'Abernon."

"Remember, Padrone, you asked for it. Sit down. I'll tell you all about it." Nick realized the effect his statement had on the former detective. Padrone sat down to hear Nick's explanation.

"It wasn't too long ago," Nick began. "A few days before the curators' meeting. I was checking through the fossils. Paleoanthropology is not really my field; it's too early for me. But I do know something about it—enough to recognize a fake reconstruction when I see one."

"You know, d'Abernon, you're not making any sense."

"No, I suppose not," Nick admitted. "It's about Samuel's great discovery. The skull he found in the Neander Valley, the one that made him famous, *Homo jekyllensis*—the so-called missing link between *Homo sapiens* and Neanderthal Man that allegedly accounted for the destructive aggressive side of our species. Samuel named it after Dr. Jekyll and Mr. Hyde—Hyde for the bad and Jekyll for the good. Trouble was Samuel was so eager to prove his theory that he got carried away. It happens sometimes in science. He combined a Neanderthal jaw with a *Homo sapiens* brain case."

"How do you know all this?" Padrone asked slowly.

"It was quite simple, really. The skull had been in its display case at the Institute for years. Completely undisturbed. Everyone assumed it was an accurate reconstruction."

"So how did *you* find out about it?"

"It was more by chance than anything. I read several recent publications on the subject. So I checked the original fossil material Samuel collected, which is still in storage at the Institute. It includes fragments from both species."

Nick saw a puzzled expression come over Padrone's face.

"Look, Joe." Nick tried to clarify what he was saying. "Most people don't realize that fossils of this kind are rarely found intact. Usually they are reconstructed out of many fragments from the same species but not necessarily from a single individual. Well, I went through all of our fragments, and I began to suspect something. I realized that Samuel had combined two distinct species into one reconstituted skull. He claimed to have found them that way. I'm not saying it was intentional fraud. I wasn't there, so I don't know exactly how it happened. It's certainly not the first time a scientist has been seduced by his own theory into arranging evidence to fit. As a matter of fact, new evidence suggests that Samuel's theory was probably correct. In 1998 the skeleton of a four-year-old child was discovered in Portugal. Its anatomy was a combination, part Neanderthal and part *Homo sapiens*. In 2003 further evidence that Neanderthal Man and *Homo sapiens* were capable of interbreeding was discovered in Ethiopia. And now it is pretty much accepted that interbreeding occurred. The problem was that Samuel couldn't wait for the evidence, and that is unacceptable in scientific circles. It can take years, even generations of exploration and research to substantiate a theory, and Samuel was in a hurry."

"And what," queried Padrone, "does all this have to do with Samuel's murder?"

"I don't know. But it's what we argued about."

"Oh, Christ. You mean you went and told him what you found out? You believed his theory but you wanted to make an issue of his methods? That's just like you."

Nick nodded silently.

"Leave it to you. You stick to your principles but forget the human side of things. Why not leave it alone?" Joe was thinking about his own behavior with Ray and his departure from the police force.

"I couldn't do that. Don't you see? Eventually someone else would have discovered the fraud. That's what the argument was about. I urged Samuel to acknowledge his error and publish a reevaluation, if not an actual retraction. He acted as if I were trying to ruin him and the Institute. He wouldn't listen to reason. It was almost as if he had forgotten how he did it. He said his life's work was based on the validity of his theory and that the reputation of the Institute would never recover from a public retraction. He got furious and threatened to destroy my career. Later that same evening, after he cooled down, he phoned me while I was working in the dark room next to my office. He said he had second thoughts and was on his way over to discuss the matter further."

"And just why was all this such a big secret? Why didn't you say so before? Save us all a lot of trouble. And what about Ruth?"

"Now listen, Padrone. Let's not start on Ruth. I didn't say anything because I wanted to give Samuel time to think. The final decision had to be his. But then he was killed, and I was arrested for his murder.

"As I said," Nick continued, "Samuel was probably right in the end. And he was dead. So since nothing could be done at that point, I figured let sleeping dogs lie. It wouldn't have helped Ruth or the Institute if Samuel's reputation were ruined. What I need now is proof that someone else had opportunity as well as motive to kill Samuel, and that whoever it was came into my office while I was in the darkroom. By the time I came out, Samuel was dead." Nick sighed, relieved to have broken his long silence.

The sense that Nick was telling the truth began to dawn on Joe Padrone. His detective's curiosity was aroused. "And what were you doing in the darkroom if you knew Samuel was on his way to your office? And what about the slide projectors?"

"When Samuel phoned, I told him I was in the middle of printing. I had been looking at old slides and noticed that one of the bronze axes in the National Museum of Crete had a bull-horn motif on the handles. Our two examples are also decorated with bulls' horns. I went into the darkroom to print an enlargement of the slide to compare it with our versions. When Samuel came down, I had another ten minutes to wait for the developer and the fixer before I could open the door. Samuel obviously sat down at my desk and ran through the slides in the carousel while he was waiting for me."

"And I suppose you didn't hear a thing?"

"Come on, Joe. You know that's a heavy door. And the slide machines make quite a racket."

Padrone did know.

"I don't think the murderer knew I was there at first," Nick went on. "When I took the print out of the fixer, I called out to Samuel that I had finished. I put it in the water bath and opened the door. I guess whoever was there must have heard me and dropped the ax. I stumbled over it and picked it up. That was a big mistake, I realize, but I didn't know what had happened. Then you came in. And that's it. That's all I know."

After a moment of silence, Padrone said, "You're either a consummate liar or a very big mistake has been made."

Nick stared at Padrone and knew that he believed him. For the first time since the murder, Nick dared to hope.

"Okay, d'Abernon, I guess you might be telling the truth. Only a complete fool would come up with a story like that at this late date. We can check your story about the skull easily enough."

"Yes, I know. But I'd still like to keep that quiet. I wanted Samuel to amend his original claim. But now, with the trial and everything that's happened, the story would unleash a new scandal. Later, when things have calmed down, I can get together with Frances Atwood and figure out the most discreet way to proceed."

"You know, you're really something. I gotta hand it to you. Here you are on trial for your life, and you're worrying about a fossil that's been dead for hundreds of thousands of years."

Nick had to smile. The atmosphere in the bleak room had changed completely. He felt a surge of energy as he realized that Padrone was on his side.

"Well, my boy." Padrone looked straight at Nick and smiled.

"You don't know it yet, but we—you and me—are going to crack this case. No one else is going to do it. Your lawyer's a nice guy, but he hasn't a clue how to proceed with your defense. Too many cards are stacked against you. The odds are terrible."

"I know," Nick said. But he felt better anyway. "It's kind of late in the game to be proving my innocence though."

"Never too late. Now, once more. let's go over the whole thing. Every detail. I want to hear it all."

When Padrone left the detention center it was 11:45 p.m. A thick blanket of snow and ice covered the ground. Well, he'd done what Ruth had asked, and he had a lot to tell her. He was going to need her help. Padrone took out his cell phone and dialed Ruth's number. After four rings he left a message. "It's me, Ruth. Joe. Call me the second you get this. It's urgent." Where the hell is she? he wondered.

Two hours and three bus rides later, Padrone was back home. He tried Ruth again. Still no answer.

CHAPTER 23

The taxi made its way slowly along Sutton Place South. The snow was still coming down and was turning to ice. Driving was hazardous. The taxi pulled to a stop in front of a tall, modern building. Ricardo paid the driver. He jumped out of the cab, gave Ruth his hand, and together they ran through the bitter cold into the warmth of the lobby.

Ruth was taken by surprise when Ricardo switched on the lights in his apartment. She hadn't known what to expect, although she did know that whatever it was, it would be tasteful and stylish. Ricardo's apartment was quite simply stunning—in a stark, minimalist way. The living room had a magnificent view across the East River onto Roosevelt Island. It extended south toward Brooklyn and north past the Queensborough Bridge.

The room was entirely white—the walls, the carpet, two sofas, and the chairs. They provided a dramatic backdrop for the impressive display of bronze and terracotta pre-Colombian figures on the glass shelves along two walls. She giggled when she realized that some of the statues were fertility figures with enormous erect phalluses. "Ricardo," she said, "is this what is meant by 'man power'?"

Ricardo smiled. "I'm glad you appreciate my collection." He gave her a brief tour of the figures, explaining their origins and the mythology behind them.

"And now," he said. "Time for the pousse-café."

Ricardo led Ruth to the bar, which was built into a mirrored alcove off the living room. He took down two snifters from a shelf and placed them on the black marble countertop. First he opened a bottle of green *crème de menthe* and poured a small amount into each glass. Then he poured a layer of apricot brandy over the back of a spoon on top of the crème de menthe. The pale-orange liqueur floated magically on the heavy, viscous layer of green. He topped this off with a third layer of Armagnac, followed by a colorless framboise.

"It's magic, Ricardo." Ruth was carried away by his infectious enthusiasm and captivated by his obvious pleasure. "It's almost too beautiful to drink."

"But you must drink it. That's part of the game. The first one to mix up the layers loses."

Ruth realized that Ricardo really was treating the whole thing like a glorious joke.

They faced each other, staring with mock seriousness into each other's eyes. As Ricardo slowly and carefully raised his glass, Ruth lifted hers and followed his example. She watched Ricardo bite his lip to keep from smiling. The glasses reached their lips. Both took a sip and swallowed. The layers in each glass remained perfectly separate. They sipped again. Quite suddenly, the game turned into some kind of ritual. It was a contest. Ruth was mesmerized by Ricardo's hypnotic gaze. As she slowly continued sipping, she began to feel the closeness of his body, and she could sense the tension in him, almost pulling her toward him. He was not smiling now. His eyes never left hers.

He lifted her glass from her hand and put it down with his on the marble counter. He bent down to kiss her. The moment his lips touched hers, Ruth felt a wave of panic. Ricardo lifted her up and carried her through the living room into his bedroom. He put her down on his enormous bed and began to caress her. Ruth was confused and afraid. This was not what she had expected or wanted. Her plan had been to remain in control and to extract information from Ricardo. Instead he was directing the evening. She tried to push him away, but her efforts to do so only increased his ardor.

"Ruth, it's time. You know you want this as much as I do."

"Please, Ricardo ..."

The telephone rang. For a moment Ruth was afraid Ricardo would let it ring. But he finally let her go. "Sorry," he gave her a kiss. "This won't take long." And he was gone.

Ruth lay for a few seconds on the bed, trying to gather her thoughts and decide what to do. She could barely make out Ricardo's voice from the living room. He was speaking German. As she began to calm down, she felt like washing her face with cold water. It would help clear her head. The drink had been a powerful one, especially on top of the champagne and wine they had had for dinner. She had to think fast.

Ruth got up and went into the bathroom. In contrast to the rest of the apartment, the bathroom was opulently decorated in brilliant color. The round, sunken tub was enormous, with Jacuzzi jets fitted along the sides. It was lapis-lazuli blue. The same white carpet as the living room covered the floor, but smaller, brightly-colored woven rugs lay on top, providing patches of warm, rich color. The shelves were filled with body lotions, creams, perfumes, and powders. The rack beside the tub held soft, thick towels in different shades of magenta, plum, and violet. Two voluminous white terrycloth robes hung from gilded hooks in the shape of swans.

Ruth leaned over the sink and splashed cold water on her face. She looked into the mirror and saw that she was pale. Dark circles were beginning to form under her eyes. The fatigue of the last few days crept over her—a reaction, she thought, to the strain and tension of the trial and to the evening with Ricardo.

She picked up a bottle of lotion, squeezed out a few drops on her hands, and rubbed it on her hands and face. She put the bottle back and searched for some aspirin in the medicine cabinet. Not finding any, she opened one of the drawers below the sink. She was confused. It was filled with syringes. She quickly shut it and opened the drawer underneath and discovered a stash of small plastic glassine packets containing a white powder.

Ruth was unsettled as well as terrified by the implications of her discovery, but she had the presence of mind to slip one of the packets into the pocket of her harem pants and push the drawer shut. It was then that she heard the menacing sound behind her.

Ruth froze, immobilized with fear. She strained to identify the noise. It seemed to come closer, inch-by-inch. Very slowly she turned around.

And there, crouched not five feet away just outside the bathroom door, was a large black-and-brown Doberman pinscher. Its ears were pressed tightly back and its teeth were bared. The growl became louder. The lips curled and globs of saliva dripped from the distended purple gums onto the carpet.

Ruth watched in horrified fascination as the animal crept forward and flexed its muscles. When it sprang, she heard herself scream. The blurred shape came for her throat. She threw herself to one side, careening into the sink.

When Ruth opened her eyes, Ricardo was kneeling beside her. "My poor Ruth," he said. "I am terribly sorry. I had no idea that Dolf had gotten out of the kitchen. He usually never bothers people, unless they are going through my things. He's a wonderful watchdog and very loyal."

Ricardo paused abruptly. "*Were* you going through my things, Ruth?"

Ruth saw his eyes narrow. She felt bruised and very afraid. She wanted to get away from Ricardo as fast as possible. But she realized that she had to keep her wits about her and be very, very careful. She suddenly knew with the utmost certainty that Ricardo was a dangerous, ruthless man.

"I guess I was, Ricardo," she said with as much innocence as she could muster. She watched Ricardo watching her. "I had a headache after that wonderful drink. I never could mix drinks. I was looking for an aspirin in the medicine cabinet. Then I heard the dog. He made such a menacing noise."

Her heart pounded. "I was terrified." She felt the tears well up. She knew they were more from fear of Ricardo than the dog, but she was relieved to see his face relax and his expression soften. He believed her story.

Only when Ricardo had shut the door of her taxi did Ruth begin to feel safe again. She took her cell phone from her purse, turned it on, and dialed.

CHAPTER 24

Sunday, November 21, 1:40 a.m.

The taxi wove its way carefully through the deserted, icy streets and pulled up in front of the Wyndham Institute. Ruth paid the driver, turned up the collar of her coat, and stepped into the chill night air. The taxi drove off, leaving Ruth with an ominous feeling of isolation. The street lamps were covered with frost. Their weak yellow light cast eerie shadows on the deep piles of snow shoveled to the edge of the pavement.

Ruth's gaze took in the dark silhouette of the Institute. There wasn't a sign of another person or even a moving car. The only sound she could hear was the wind howling across Central Park and lashing the trees in the courtyard of the Institute. Their dark branches writhed against the cloudy, moonlit sky.

A shiver ran down Ruth's spine. She was cold and exhausted after her evening with Ricardo. She inhaled deeply, wrapped her coat closely around herself, and made her way over the bank of frozen snow onto the sidewalk. Trying to find her keys at the bottom of her purse made her realize that her fingers were numb and stiff. She inserted the key awkwardly into the lock on the gate and turned it with difficulty. The heavy wrought-iron bars slowly swung forward on their frozen hinges.

Ruth slipped around the gate and leaned against it until she heard it click shut. The sound was comforting. She felt safer with the gate locked behind her.

The snow in the courtyard was white and clean in the moonlight. A path had been cleared from the gate to the heavy glass doors of the Institute. Ruth hurried along the path and climbed the imposing stairs to the entrance. She turned her keys over in the palm of her glove, found the right one, and let herself in. She shut the heavy doors behind her, relieved to be out of the cold. Turning left, Ruth passed the elevator and hurried down the flight of stairs leading to the basement. When she saw the light under the door, she smiled and began to relax.

"It's me, Peter," she called out. "Let me in.

The door opened at once. With a sweeping bow and flourish of his right arm, Peter Ryan gestured Ruth into his lab.

"How smashingly unexpected to see you, my dear," he said in an exaggerated upper-class British accent. "You certainly sounded upset on the phone. What on earth is the matter? And to what do I owe the pleasure of your company? It is kind of late," Peter observed.

Ruth went straight past Peter and sank into one of his two motley armchairs. She propped her feet on the ottoman.

"Just wait until you hear, Peter," she said with false cheerfulness. Then her mood changed. "I can't tell you how reassuring it is to be here. I need some … help." She choked on the word as she began to cry. Peter's figure, blurred by the tears, came toward her. He knelt by the side of the chair.

"What is it, Ruth?" He put his arm around her and pulled her head against his chest, stroking her hair. With his free hand he reached into his trouser pocket and pulled out an enormous red-and-white checked handkerchief. He dabbed her eyes. "Here," he said, "blow your nose like a good girl."

Ruth did as she was told.

"God, Peter," was all she could say. But she felt better.

"What has happened? Is it Nick?"

"No, it's not Nick. It's …" she paused. "I don't know what to think. I was terrified."

"Tell Uncle Peter all about it." Peter stood up and settled into the other armchair. "I am all ears." He stretched out his legs and put his feet up on an old crate that doubled as a table. He took his pipe from the ashtray, tapped out the burnt remnants of tobacco from the bowl, and refilled it.

"I don't even know where to begin."

"Try the beginning. The facts. Just tell me all the facts," Peter was devoted to Sherlock Holmes. Facts came first and theories after.

"Yes, all right." Ruth paused again. "Well, I guess the beginning was when Ricardo asked me to dinner. I would never have accepted but—"

"Don't tell me you are interested in the Colombian lothario now that Nick is behind bars."

"Of course not, Peter. You know better than that."

"Then why?"

"I guess it was stupid, but I wanted to see if I could find something out. You know, something more about what had been going on around here that might lead to my father's murderer."

"That can be dangerous, Ruth. A bad idea."

"Ricardo always seems so charming, and for part of the evening he really *was* charming. I must have had too much to drink." Ruth remembered the pousse-café. "Maybe he was testing me as much as I was him," she said almost to herself.

Peter decided to wait. He saw Ruth's exhaustion. She was deathly pale. The dark circles under her tearstained eyes made them seem unusually bright. But she is still beautiful, Peter thought. She was like a pre-Raphaelite modern: delicate, fragile, and vulnerable. He felt a wave of compassion and had to fight an overwhelming urge to take her into his arms right then and there. He had always hoped that Ruth would someday turn to him, and here she was. He savored the moment. But he would make no advances unless she made it clear that she was receptive to them. To be rejected by her was unthinkable. He had, in fact, wanted Ruth from their first meeting, when he had come to the Institute at the urging of her father. She should have been his. She was rightfully his. And she would be his once d'Abernon was taken care of.

Peter puffed slowly on his pipe, knowing he had to wait until she was ready to talk but curious nonetheless. What had Ricardo, that arrogant lady-killer, done to put Ruth in such a state? Peter was angry but relieved that Ruth now seemed aware of Ricardo's shortcomings. That made one less suitor, two with Nick out of the way.

"I went back to Ricardo's apartment. I ... that is, he went to answer the telephone." Ruth did not mention the bedroom. "He made this incredible drink from different liqueurs and I guess it hit me. So I went into the bathroom to splash some cold water on my face and hunt for an aspirin. It's an incredible bathroom, a sybarite's paradise."

"Doesn't surprise me in the least," Peter muttered.

Ruth ignored his comment. "I opened a drawer. It was full of syringes. And then I found this." She pulled out the small plastic package and tossed in into Peter's lap.

"I don't know why I took it, but I was suspicious. Just then I heard an awful noise. I looked around and saw a huge, black dog, a Doberman. It was crouching in the doorway and growling fiercely. I froze and stood there like an idiot as it slouched toward me." Ruth leaned forward, gripping the frayed arms of the chair. She was rigid with the memory of her fear. "I don't quite know what happened, but I saw the dog moving. Then it sprang and I screamed. The next thing I remember is Ricardo questioning me. He asked if I had been going through his things. He said the dog was trained to attack only if someone was invading his privacy. Ricardo's expression was threatening; he looked ruthless. His voice and face were completely altered, taut and hard. Especially his eyes.

"I lied, of course. I didn't mention the packets. I only said I was searching for an aspirin in the medicine cabinet. I guess he believed me because he became his old self again. But something is going on, Peter. Isn't that heroin in the plastic?" Ruth slumped against the back of her chair. She was exhausted.

Peter held up the glassine packet to the light. "Syringes, you say?"

"Yes."

"Well, I think it's safe to assume that this is indeed heroin. I probably should test it just to make sure, though."

"I thought it was. But Ricardo is hardly the type to take drugs. I don't understand."

"It was pretty stupid of him," Peter said, "to leave stuff like this lying about for unsuspecting ladies to discover. Careless, very careless, I would say. But let's be certain. You relax while I play chemist."

Peter walked over to his lab counter. He opened the packet of white powder very carefully with his Swiss army knife. He poured a small amount of the powder into an evaporating dish. He licked his right index finger, dipped it into the dish, and tasted it. He didn't need to do any further tests.

"It's heroin all right." Peter turned to look at Ruth.

Her cheek was resting against the back of the chair. Her eyes were closed and her dark curls fell in confusion over her forehead. She was breathing regularly.

Peter smiled. He tiptoed to the closet, took out the blanket he kept there for his all-nighters, and tucked it carefully around Ruth. He kissed her on the forehead and sat down to wait.

CHAPTER 25

Sunday, November 21, 10:30 a.m.

R uth awoke with a start. At first she had no idea where she was. But then she saw Peter.

He smiled. "Coffee?" he asked, pushing himself up from his chair.

Ruth watched him fill the dented, aluminum kettle and set in on the tripod over a lighted Bunsen burner. "Yes, please. What time is it, Peter? How long have I been here?"

"It's 10:30 on a fine but cold Sunday morning," he said, pouring boiling water into a chipped mug and adding a heaping spoonful of instant Nescafé. "You had a very good sleep. Must have been exhausted."

"Am I dreaming, Peter, or did I tell you, or did you tell me, that Ricardo's packet contained heroin?"

"You did not dream it, Ruth. Milk?"

"Yes, please. Lots."

Peter handed Ruth the steaming mug. She took it gratefully.

"My head doesn't feel great," Ruth admitted sheepishly.

"I have just the thing." Peter removed a small glass bottle from

one of the lab shelves. He filled a beaker with cold water and poured
in a good measure of tiny white crystals from the bottle, stirring the
brew with the end of the coffee spoon.

"This is my own recipe for 'hair of the dog.' It never fails." He
brought the foaming concoction to Ruth. "Drink it down all at once
or it won't work. In ten minutes you'll be your old self again."

"Thanks, Peter. How lucky to end up in a chemistry lab on *this*
particular morning." Ruth drained the glass and settled down to
sip her coffee.

"I still don't know what's going on, though," she said. "Do you
think there could be a connection between Ricardo, the heroin,
and my father's murder? I just know Nick didn't do it. What do
you think?"

"I really have no idea, Ruth. Are you suggesting that Ricardo
might be the killer?"

"I guess I am." Ruth was suddenly on her feet. "I better call Joe.
That's what I should do. My cell phone's battery is gone. May I use
your phone?"

"Of course."

Ruth sat at Peter's desk. As she punched in Joe Padrone's number,
she glanced over the mess of papers, forms, unwashed coffee mugs,
and overflowing ashtrays littering Peter's chaotic desk.

"Joe, it's Ruth." Ruth heard the sigh of relief at the other end
of the line.

"Jesus, Ruth. Where the hell have you been? I tried to call you
all night long. I tried again this morning. I was about to call the
hospitals."

"I'm sorry, Joe. It's a long story. I don't know if it will help Nick,
but it just might. Can we talk?"

"I'll say we can. I have a lot to tell you. I saw Nick last night.
Can't say I wanted to, as you know. Only went because you insisted.
But he finally told me what happened during the argument with

your father, and you should know it too. I have to eat crow, Ruth, but I am pretty sure he's innocent."

"Do you mean it? That's wonderful! What did he tell you?"

"Look, Ruth, not over the phone. We have to move fast if we're going to help your fiancé." The last two words were said in a mocking tone. "I promised I'd go see him again this morning. Why don't you come with me and surprise him? Which reminds me, where are you?"

"I'm in Peter's lab. I got here late last night. I found something in Ricardo's apartment and I wanted Peter to identify it for me."

"In Ricardo's apartment? What did you find?"

"Heroin, Joe." Ruth paused. "I don't know what it means."

"It means we have a lot to talk about. Stay put. I'll be there in twenty minutes."

Ruth heard the phone click. She replaced the receiver and turned toward Peter.

He saw that the color had returned to her cheeks.

"Joe doesn't think Nick's guilty, Peter." Her smile was radiant. "I wonder what made him change his mind."

True to his word, Joe Padrone arrived twenty minutes later. He thanked Peter for taking care of Ruth as they set off for the long trip to Riker's Island.

CHAPTER 26

Sunday, November 21, 11:45 a.m.

Nadim answered his cell phone.

"We have one more problem to clear up." It was the same disguised monotonous voice as before.

"What now?"

"Montoya knows about the plan to bomb the Institute. He has to be eliminated as quickly as possible before he alerts the police."

"How the hell did he find out?"

"Are you questioning my authority? You know the penalty for disloyalty."

CHAPTER 27

Sunday, November 21, 2:00 p.m.

R uth was not at all prepared for what she encountered either outside or inside the detention center on Riker's Island. The locking and unlocking of the gates unnerved her; then her handbag was searched and a metal detector scanned her entire body. The guards seemed to have left their humanity outside the gates. They performed their routines efficiently, unthinkingly, with stony, bored, and hostile expressions.

The bare visitors' room, even more claustrophobic than the one at the courthouse, depressed Ruth. Then Nick arrived in his shapeless, orange prison suit. He stood at the door, hesitating.

"Look," Padrone said as he broke the silence, "I'll take five while you lovebirds straighten out whatever has to be straightened out." Joe disappeared into the corridor. The door slammed behind him.

Ruth's gaze met Nick's.

He held his arms out to her. "Come on, darling," he said. "I think it's time I told you about Lillian so you don't hold it against me for the whole of our married life." He smiled.

It was the same old jaunty, amused smile Ruth remembered from before the trial. He looked different too, bigger and stronger, more like the old Nick. He has hope now, she thought, with a huge sense of relief. She felt Nick's arms close tightly around her. He kissed her forehead, her ear, and then her mouth. After a few moments she pushed him away.

"Okay, Mr. d'Abernon. It's just lucky I love you as much as I do. You have some pretty fancy explaining to do. I suggest you start now."

"So do you, darling. Why are you wearing that extraordinary outfit at this time of the morning?"

Ruth had completely forgotten that she was still in the harem pants left over from her date with Ricardo. "Never mind that now, Nick. Let's hear it."

"Very well. It all started with a young archaeology student at Stanford by the name of Nicholas d'Abernon."

When Padrone returned, he saw that Nick and Ruth were deep in conversation. Their expressions told him that all was well.

"Now that you have settled your personal affairs," Joe said, "we better figure out how we are going to get Nick out of here. From my years on the force"—Padrone shot Nick a warning glance—"I know that drug trafficking, if that's what Montoya is up to, can lead to some pretty complicated, violent, and bizarre events. Tell the story again, Ruth."

Ruth began to describe her evening with Ricardo once again. Padrone noticed that she glossed over a few of the more suggestive details she mentioned on the way over. Just as well, he thought, male vanity being what it is.

When she finished, they realized that they didn't have all that much to go on. But they had more than before. As a first move, they agreed that Padrone and Ruth would search Ricardo's office.

Sunday night was a perfect time for snooping around without fear of interruption. Ruth knew that Ricardo would be attending the eagerly awaited, black-tie gala at the Egyptian embassy to celebrate the birthday of the prime minister.

CHAPTER 28

Sunday, November 21, 4:45 p.m.

At 4:45 p.m., the closing bell of the Wyndham Institute rang. The remaining visitors shuffled toward the entrance. When the iron courtyard gates clanged shut behind the last stragglers, the security guards turned their attention to the elaborate evening procedure of activating the alarm system. One of the advantages of Padrone's system was its eclectic design, which combined the most effective aspects of the different types already on the market with a few original devices of his own.

Every window frame and door was wired with magnets imbedded into the wall. At certain points under the marble tiles in the entrance hall and display rooms and under the oak floorboards of the upper stories, Padrone had installed pressure pads that would instantly alert security to any intruder. Each office was wired in the same way. In addition, the walls and desks were equipped with panic buttons connected to the security desk in the main hall and to the transistors carried by each guard.

Every file cabinet and display case was wired to the main system. The connections could be turned on or off with a coded key. The basement storage area and top floor library were activated by an entirely separate system. On the orders of Samuel Wyndham each curator knew the ins and outs of all the security devices so that they were free to work on weekends, holidays, and evenings.

Ricardo Montoya arrived at the Institute just before closing time. He rarely worked on weekends, and this weekend was no exception. He was dressed in a dinner jacket, starched white evening shirt, and maroon, velvet bowtie. He was on his way to the Egyptian embassy. The reception began at seven, but first he had an important meeting in his office. He hurried through the spacious entrance hall, past the Egyptian and Mesopotamian collections. As he entered the Far Eastern department, Ricardo was surprised to find Lillian Nakamura examining a Chinese cauldron. Charlie Wei stood beside her, busily taking notes while she dictated. On the floor lay a second cauldron, similar to the one whose provenance Peter Ryan had pronounced a forgery during his testimony. Lillian was so absorbed that she failed to notice Ricardo pause and stare. Charlie noticed. He tapped Lillian's shoulder and she looked up.

"Hello, there." Ricardo waved, a slight, cynical smile on his lips. "Are you stealing the cauldron in the case or substituting the forgery on the floor?"

Lillian threw Ricardo a look of venom.

He laughed out loud and left without another word. When Ricardo reached his office, he unlocked the door, went in, and sat down at his desk to wait for Jorn Hill.

Frances Atwood had decided to stay late at the Institute.

A shipment of skull and bone fragments had arrived that afternoon by FedEx from South Africa, and she was eager to begin examining them. Frances had been informed that the specimens contained several skulls that had been smashed on the left side in precisely the same way as the skulls found by Raymond Dart. She believed that this new evidence would provide further corroboration of Dart's theory that man was innately aggressive. She was making mental notes for an article on the new findings.

Frances was jolted from her thoughts by the telephone.

"Hello, Dr. Atwood. I'm so glad I caught you," boomed the cheery voice of Robert Braithwaite, her biographer.

He was the last person Frances expected and certainly the least welcome. She was unable to disguise her chagrin.

"Look, Dr. Atwood," Braithwaite persisted, "I know we agreed to give the book a rest during the trial, but something has come up and I need your help to clarify a point. It won't take long." He tried to reassure her. "It's only a minor discrepancy."

"Very well," said Frances wearily. Her enthusiasm for the new skulls dampened. "What is the discrepancy?"

"It's about your husband's death," Braithwaite began cautiously.

"Yes?" Frances prayed that her voice did not betray the panic welling up inside her.

"Well, I was going over my notes and records," explained her biographer. "And I noticed the local African coroner's report indicates that your husband fell into a cave and died instantly. In my notes I have a reference to your efforts to pull him out. There was no indication of a struggle at the cave entrance; the surface rim was apparently intact. I do apologize for bringing this up, but one has to be thorough."

"Yes, of course one does," Frances replied. "I quite understand. But actually, I'm with someone at the moment," she lied. "Could we discuss this later? I'll call you back." Frances hung up before her caller had a chance to reply.

Frances Atwood was a changed woman. Her body sagged as if she had aged rapidly in the course of the phone call. She pushed back her chair, rose slowly, and locked her door. She opened the bottom drawer of the filing cabinet where her excavation records were stored. At the back was a bottle of Johnny Walker. It was half full.

By the time Jorn Hill entered the Wyndham Institute, the alarm system was on and he had to use his coded keys. He nodded to the security guard at the entrance and proceeded to Ricardo's office. The door was slightly ajar. Jorn pushed it open and strode inside.

"Here it is." Jorn flung his words at Montoya as he threw a wad of hundred-dollar bills on the desk.

Ricardo folded his arms, leaned back in his chair, and stared at Jorn. Except for a slightly raised eyebrow, his expression remained impassive in the face of Jorn's bravado.

"So which Greek vase did you sell to get this?" Ricardo asked sardonically. "I saw your pal Ted outside the court room. I would say his habit is getting out of hand, wouldn't you?"

Ricardo counted the money slowly and methodically.

Neither spoke. The only sound was the rustling of the bills. When Ricardo had counted the last one, he held it between his fingers before dropping it on the neat pile stacked in front of him. He looked inquiringly at Jorn.

"You're short, Hill, short by quite a lot." Ricardo's eyes narrowed. His tone was menacing. "What are we going to do about it?" He reached for the telephone. "Perhaps we should ask Elizabeth? Would you like that, Jorn?"

Charles Dudley sat glumly at his desk, clearing up the paperwork that had piled up since Wyndham's death. His thoughts turned to Nigel's arrival in New York. So far he had avoided dealing with him, even though Margaret kept trying to get them together for her own perverse enjoyment. Above all, Dudley did not want Nigel to run into Montoya. In his alcoholic haze, Nigel was capable of saying anything. He might brag about having written Dudley's thesis.

Charles decided he would go to his club and relax with a few rounds of backgammon. The telephone rang. It was Margaret.

"Darling," she said in her brittle public voice, "Nigel and I are on our way over to the Institute. Do tell security to expect us." She hung up before he had time to reply.

Nadim Tariq passed security on the way to his office.

CHAPTER 29

Sunday, November 21, 6:40 p.m.

"You go straight to Montoya's office and wait for me there. Here's the key." Padrone and Ruth had just entered the Wyndham Institute. It was 6:40 p.m. Padrone handed Ruth the pass key to all the offices. "I'm going to run a complete security check on this place," he said. "And don't worry. I'll use the video screen in the central office. As long as there is a light on, I can see every room from there."

"Okay, Joe," Ruth said. "I'll see you in a few minutes."

"Right. And, Ruth, remember, if you have any problems, just push the alarm button on Montoya's desk. Be sure to turn on the light when you enter."

Ruth detected the warning in Joe's voice. She set out resolutely for Ricardo's office, secure in the knowledge he would be on his way to the Egyptian embassy.

Joe Padrone contacted the security guards on night duty. They reported that all was well. Padrone headed for the central security control panel located on the first floor. He checked the screen for Montoya's office. It was dark. Ruth obviously wasn't there yet. He pressed a button and the camera picked up Ruth walking down the corridor toward the office. Padrone went to join her.

Ruth felt a shudder down her spine as she proceeded through the dimly lit hallway. She could not shake off the terror of the previous night. Nor could she forget the memory of her father's brutal murder in Nick's office, which was directly opposite Ricardo's. She was grateful that Nick's door was closed.

What did surprise her, however, was that Ricardo's door was slightly ajar. She stood absolutely still. She had been certain he would be on his way to the embassy by this time. The only sound was her own shallow breathing and the rapid pounding of her heart. She held her breath. Nothing. She told herself to stay calm, but some instinct warned her of another human presence.

Ruth was a few feet from Ricardo's door. She stepped forward and then stopped. She listened. Still no sound. She took another three steps. Come on, Joe, she pleaded silently. The office was pitch dark. One more step and Ruth felt for the light switch. She flicked it on and screamed.

She didn't know how long it was before Joe Padrone ran to her side.

"Oh my God!" he shouted at once.

Ricardo Montoya's body leaned back in his desk chair. His severed head had been placed at the center of his desk. His eyes were wide open, staring, and his lips were twisted into a grimace of hatred and surprise. He had been decapitated, and an expanding pool of blood spread across his desk. Blood poured from his neck, staining his white shirt. His right hand lay on the desk, gripping his gold cigarette lighter.

Padrone put his arm around Ruth and turned her away from the gruesome tableau. He tried to calm her as his eyes searched the room for clues. Nothing made any sense. Padrone glanced at the floor beside the desk and saw something that didn't fit. He picked up what seemed to be a cigarette butt. He sniffed it. It smelled like tobacco, but something else was mixed with it. Puzzled, Padrone put it in his jacket pocket, pressed the alarm, and ushered Ruth from Montoya's office.

CHAPTER 30

Monday, November 23, 10:57 a.m.

Nick paced back and forth in the small, bleak visitors' room on Riker's Island. He was waiting anxiously for Padrone and Ruth. He knew about Ricardo and was worried. He wanted to see for himself that Ruth was all right.

The door opened and Ruth rushed into his arms. Padrone hung back discreetly. Nick leaned down and pressed his cheek against Ruth's dark curls. "Poor Ruth," he said. "How do you feel this morning? I worried about you all night."

Nick smiled. "But I knew Joe would take care of you."

Ruth looked at Padrone. "And he did," she said with a grin. "A little Scotch and a lot of talk did wonders!" She freed herself from Nick's embrace, unbuttoned her heavy coat, and draped it over the back of a wooden chair. "Ricardo's murder was horrible, Nick. But, as Joe says, at least it casts suspicion on someone besides you."

"What about that, Joe?" Nick asked. "Why can't I get out of here now? Can they still keep me here after what happened to Ricardo?"

"You'll have to be patient a bit longer. Rogers will do his best to get you out Wednesday when court reconvenes. But there's a hell of a lot of red tape, and then there's Crawford. He's not going to like this. He's under pressure to keep you right where you are. My pals at the mayor's office tell me he's not quite the golden boy he was at the beginning of the trial. Seems the mayor wanted the whole thing wrapped up fast so it wouldn't interfere with his plans for the exhibition dinner. Crawford assured him there was no contest, said that Rogers didn't have a chance. As of now, Crawford has been severely rapped on the knuckles for failing to do his homework." Padrone smiled and so did Nick and Ruth.

"Anyway," Joe continued, "Crawford will probably argue that Montoya's murder has nothing to do with Samuel's, that it's not unusual for brutal murders to be imitated. It's the copycat syndrome. And I can tell you from my own experience on the force that he has a point. So, you may have to stick in here for longer than you'd like, Nick, but there is something you can do right this minute, something that may shorten the time considerably."

Padrone reached into his jacket pocket and pulled out a white envelope that had been folded several times. He sat down at the bare table, gesturing to Nick and Ruth to join him. He carefully opened the envelope and shook out the contents.

"This is what I found on the floor of Montoya's office," Joe said, picking up the stub. "I know that Ricardo smoked, but he wasn't one to throw a butt on the floor. Too fastidious for that, and too fastidious to leave it lying there. I conclude, therefore, that the person who dropped it was the last person to see Ricardo alive. Hence, the killer." Padrone paused, gratified by the attention his statement was receiving. He slipped back easily into the role of police detective.

"Take a good look, Nick. It's no ordinary cigarette—maybe not just the thing to bring into a prison, but the guys here all know me. Hand-rolled yes, but there's more here than tobacco." Padrone drew his black address book from his hip pocket. He tore out one of the back pages and put it on the table. He placed the butt on the paper. With a small pocket knife, he slit the butt along its length. He spread it apart carefully so as not to lose any of the contents.

"It doesn't take a genius to see that this is tobacco," Padrone said, pointing to the dried brown leaves. "But there is something else as well, and I can't identify it."

With the tip of his knife, Padrone eased out a few grains of white powder mixed in with the tobacco filaments. "It's not cocaine, and it's not heroin. I don't know what it is. But I do know something." He looked at Nick. "Something that I think you two know even more about, now that I begin to put two and two together."

Padrone was silent. He stared directly at Nick. His eyes were hard and questioning, his expression businesslike and determined.

Nick was taken aback. He felt threatened by Padrone, as if he were being accused. His body tensed.

"What is it, Joe? I don't know what you are talking about."

"I'm talking about Ted Curtis, Nick. I'm talking about those axes and about your not signing them out." Padrone stopped a moment then resumed. "I didn't think much about it during the trial, but Hill's testimony didn't ring true even then. He was obviously holding something back. And so were you! When I thought about it, I realized that it's not like you to take things from the storerooms without signing for them, against your principles. Eh, Ruth?"

Nick breathed a sigh of relief.

Padrone continued. "And then there was the scene I witnessed after the court adjourned on Friday. Ted Curtis and Jorn Hill, an unlikely couple, I admit, but very much a couple—at least for the brief moments I saw them together. And you'll never believe what they were arranging, or would you, Nick? A rendezvous at the Institute! Curtis didn't look in very good shape to me. On the skids, I would say. Sweating, shaking, all the signs of a head in need of a fix. Poor Elizabeth, it was her arrival that broke up the happy couple. So, my boy," said Padrone, fixing Nick with a steely gaze, "what exactly did go on in that storeroom, and what do you know about Curtis? I have the pieces; you put them together for us."

Nick described the scene in the storeroom, along with his confusion, disbelief, and then anger at Jorn for his damaging testimony. Obviously Ted and Jorn had been lovers for some time. Nick remembered several chance encounters he had had with the two of them over the last eighteen months. He hadn't thought anything of them at the time, but he certainly did now.

"After I left the storeroom, I remember wondering how Jorn could have gotten himself involved with Curtis," Nick said. "Curtis is nothing as far as I can see. But then my tastes run in different directions." Nick reached across the table and ruffled Ruth's hair. "So, to ape the master sleuth in our midst, I would say that Jorn could easily have found himself in the position of being blackmailed. And if Joe is right and Curtis is an addict, poor old Jorn is probably footing the bill. In which case we have just stepped on a hornet's nest."

"You're learning fast, Nick. Sure you don't want to give up all the bullshit in the museum world and enter the real world of men like us cops?"

"None of that macho stuff, Joe," said Ruth. "You don't really believe it anyway." She turned to Nick. "Are you suggesting that Jorn was the one stealing from the Institute and using the money to finance Curtis's habit?"

"Yes, darling, I am. So what do you think? Because if I'm right, we have another piece to fit into the puzzle. And that piece is Ricardo Guzman Montoya. Our cozy couple might very well have been a not-so-cozy threesome. And what does any of this have to do with Samuel's murder?" Nick put his hand over Ruth's.

Joe explained. "Montoya was running heroin. That much I do know. He smuggled it from South America. Heaven knows he was

down there all the time. He had the right connections too. None of
the authorities would ever have tried to stop him. And if there was
ever any doubt, Ruth's discovery of his syringes and glassine packets
confirms it."

"But how did he—" began Ruth.

"In the artifacts. He hid the drugs in the figurines. Remember
that original works of art are pretty much ignored by customs, since
there is no import tax on them.

"But after I alerted the cops, they searched his apartment. They
would have anyway after his murder. The bags Ruth found were
nothing compared to what the cops uncovered. What you found
was a recreational stash for his personal enjoyment. The cops found
thirty-six pounds of the pure stuff, uncut heroin. Most of it was in
the hollowed-out pre-Colombian statues. Quite a collection I hear."
Padrone gave Ruth a meaningful glance. "One ideally suited to our
late lady-killer, I am told. Besides the heroin, which on the current
market would sell for something in excess of five million, there was
$642,000 in cash."

Nick let out a whistle of surprise.

"Banknotes." Padrone went on. "Piled in a closet. So Montoya
was clearly onto a good thing."

Joe leaned back and continued in the practiced manner of an
experienced police officer. "The questions before us are: First, did
Montoya deal in anything besides heroin, anything that might
explain this cigarette butt?" Padrone picked up the torn page from his
address book with the butt on it and eased it back into the envelope.
"Maybe Montoya was dispatched by a dissatisfied customer," he said
with a cynical smile." Second question: is there any reason to believe
that Montoya sold drugs to anyone at the Institute? I'm thinking of
Jorn and Curtis, of course.

"When we have the answers to these questions, we will be well
on our way to getting Nick out of his jumpsuit. So, what I propose

is that we enlist Peter Ryan's help and ask him to analyze our new evidence. I can't very well ask my pals on the force to do it since I removed it from the scene of the crime. And I don't particularly want to join Nick in here.

"Peter has a soft spot for you, Ruth, and I am sure he would do it if you asked."

Ruth nodded. "Okay, I can do that."

"In the meantime, I will head over to Montoya's apartment and see what I can find out about his bank account and telephone records. I'm sure there's a connection between Hill, Montoya, and Curtis. But we need solid proof."

"Sounds good to me," Nick said. "Are you sure you are up to it, Ruth?"

"Positively." She nodded vigorously. "After Ricardo, anything seems easy. But I hate leaving you here."

"It won't be for long," Joe said. "Read a good book, Nick. We'll call you later. You're nine-tenths out of here." Padrone thumped Nick on the back. "Hang in there," he said as he and Ruth departed.

CHAPTER 31

Tuesday, November 23, 3:45 p.m.

Nick was reading a good book just as Joe had suggested. He had gone to the prison library after Ruth and Padrone left the previous day and chose *The Picture of Dorian Gray* by Oscar Wilde. He thought its macabre, surreal subject matter fit his situation perfectly. He had read it as a boy and was fascinated by the contrast between the eternally youthful and beautiful Dorian and his portrait, which grew progressively uglier and more deformed with each act of cruelty and debauchery. Nick rested the dog-eared volume on his chest. He lay stretched out on his narrow prison cot, his feet dangling over the end. His head was propped up on the single hard pillow.

Nick couldn't concentrate. He had to force himself to focus on each word, or else he found himself losing track of the story.

Dorian Gray's deterioration under the influence of cynical, worldly-wise Lord Henry Wotton changed him from a gentle, loving young man into a dissolute misanthrope. But the only tangible evidence of his moral decline lay in his portrait, which exerted a horrible fascination on Dorian: "He would creep upstairs to the locked room, open the door with the key that never left him now, and stand, with a mirror, in front of the portrait that Basil Hallward had painted of him, looking now at the evil and aging face on the canvas, and now at the fair young face that laughed back at him from the polished glass. The very sharpness of the contrast used to quicken his sense of pleasure. He grew more and more enamoured of his own beauty, more and more interested in the corruption of his own soul."

Something in Wilde's description struck Nick. As he read on, now riveted by the story, he became convinced that Wilde was providing him with an important clue. He suddenly leapt from the bed and pounded on his cell door, yelling for the guard. He knew without a shadow of a doubt who had murdered Samuel Wyndham.

After what seemed like an eternity, a guard arrived looking bored and annoyed.

"What's the racket for, d'Abernon?" the guard said without the least sign of interest.

"I've got to make a phone call. It's a matter of life and death!"

"That's what they all say." The guard went through his keys one by one with excruciating slowness until he found the key that opened to Nick's cell. He handled it for a moment before inserting it in the lock.

It was all Nick could do to stop himself from screaming obscenities at him. He knew the guard was stalling on purpose, a functionary's revenge for a demeaning job. Nick realized that if he made the slightest complaint, he would be at the man's mercy and Ruth and Padrone might very easily die. So he kept quiet. The only sign of his intense agitation was the perspiration forming on his forehead and his clenched jaw.

The door to his cell finally swung open. Nick stopped himself from rushing through it. He knew that any sudden movement would

CHAPTER 32

Tuesday, November 23, 4:05 p.m.

"Peter? Thank goodness you are finally home! I've been trying to reach you all afternoon." Ruth was enormously relieved.

"The cops have been questioning us all day. I just got back."

"Listen, I really need your help again. Will you do me a big favor?"

"Of course, Ruth, you know I will." Peter sensed the desperation in her voice. Of course he would help her, and for the second time in a few days. Maybe things were at last going his way. For a brief moment he allowed himself to think of Ruth as his. D'Abernon had never been good enough for her. "Just name it," he said.

Ruth was breathless. "Can you meet me at the Institute? In your lab, I mean. It's about Ricardo. Joe found something else and he wants you to check it out."

"Be glad to," said Peter, concealing his disappointment. Once again it wasn't that Ruth wanted him, she wanted his services. But better that than nothing … and who knows? "I'll be there in half an hour."

"Thanks, Peter. I knew I could count on you."

If you only knew how much, thought Peter hanging up the phone.

Peter was in the lab when Ruth arrived.

"Come on in," he said expansively, taking Ruth's down jacket and cashmere scarf. The freezing evening air had put two bright pink patches of color in Ruth's cheeks, and her large dark eyes glistened with urgency. "What's the hurry?" Peter asked. Ruth looked beautiful.

She fumbled in her purse. "It's this," she said quickly. She handed Peter the envelope containing the half-smoked cigarette.

"Looks like pot to me," Peter said. "Smells like it too." He sniffed it slowly. "You say this came from Ricardo's office?"

"Yes," Ruth replied anxiously. "Joe found it. You know, when we discovered the …" Ruth shuddered at the memory of Ricardo's headless torso, unable to finish her sentence.

"Do the police know about it?"

"No," Ruth admitted. "Joe didn't know exactly what it was. At first he thought it was just an ordinary cigarette and he asked me who among the curators smoked. We know Ricardo did, but we couldn't imagine him throwing a butt on the floor or leaving it there. Joe noticed that it had been hand-rolled, and when he unrolled it, he discovered a small amount of white powder sprinkled on the tobacco."

"Trust Padrone," Peter laughed. "That's tampering with evidence, you know."

"Yes, I suppose it is. But please, Peter. Joe thought we could work faster than the police if we did it ourselves. We have so little time, you see, because Nick's defense starts tomorrow."

It was still Nick then, Peter realized. He barely admitted to himself the pain caused by Ruth's words. He turned away, reached for his pipe, and pounded it harder than necessary against the laboratory sink. When he turned back to Ruth, he was his genial self, the pipe in his mouth, exhaling billows of sweet-smelling smoke.

"I conclude from the flurry of activity," Peter said, trying to sound cheerful, "that your confidence in old Nick has been restored, and that all is well between you?"

Ruth nodded and smiled.

"Too bad," he said lightly. "Sort of closes out the field for the rest of us. And what is our friendly former detective, plodding Padrone, doing for our incarcerated hero while you are here with me?"

Ruth couldn't help laughing, even though she felt a tiny bit disloyal to Padrone. "He's gone to Ricardo's apartment to check with the police. They are still searching it. Please, Peter, can you identify what's in that cigarette? Joe thinks if we can find out what it is it will lead us to the murderer."

"Far be it from me to impede the galloping white horse of our knight in shining armor." Peter bowed gallantly. "I will get right on the case, my dear Watson. But it will take a little time. I'll have to run a couple of tests. In the meantime, make yourself comfortable and join me in a beer."

Impatient as Ruth was, the idea of a cold beer appealed to her enormously. She had slept fitfully the last two nights, and her last substantial meal had been dinner with Ricardo. Suddenly she realized just how tired and hungry she was. "It sounds wonderful," she said as she sat down in Peter's old armchair.

Peter removed two beers from his well-stocked fridge, placed them on the sink counter, and poured them into the two mugs he removed from the cabinet above.

"Thank you," said Ruth as he handed her a beer.

"Cheers." Peter raised his mug. "And now to work." He turned to his test tubes, leaving Ruth to her beer.

It was not long before Ruth felt the effect of the drink. Her muscles began to relax and a pleasant, drowsy sensation enveloped her. She felt as if she were floating. As she began to nod, she tried to get hold of herself. This was no time to fall asleep, welcome though sleep would be. Peter might have the solution any minute now and she would have to leave right away. Ruth decided she would force herself to walk around the lab and stay awake.

A silent panic seized her. She was unable to move. For a brief moment she was puzzled.

And then Peter turned around.

Ruth saw his changed expression. His eyes were hard and his jaw was clenched.

"I'm sorry, Ruth," he said, "but I had no choice. You came too close to the truth. It's Padrone's fault, you know. Sending you here, I mean. He, of all people, should have known better!"

Peter stared into Ruth's eyes as they darted frantically around the lab searching for some means of escape.

"You should relax, you know. There's nothing you can do. I put a muscle relaxant in the beer. It won't wear off until it's too late." Peter shrugged then he continued.

"You should have understood, Ruth. I have watched you since the day I came to the Institute. You were sixteen years old, a skinny, shy, beautiful, delicate child." Peter's face softened at the memory. "You hardly ever said a word. I loved your confusion and your courage even then. I watched and waited, hoping you would eventually realize who loved you the most. The only one who could love you the way you deserve. I thought I had plenty of time, that I had to give *you* time. I wanted you to learn by yourself as you changed into what you are now. I searched for signs that I was wrong about you and you were like every other woman I had known. But I never found them."

Peter paused. Ruth watched in terror, confused by his words, suddenly understanding things she had always been vaguely aware of but had dismissed out of hand. Now she wished that Peter would stop staring at her.

"Every woman I have ever known was a predator, taker, user, and discarder. Like the female praying mantis who bites off the male's head the moment he enters her. What does she care? The headless fool continues his work until the end. She is satisfied. He is dead!" Peter's agitation was mounting.

"Women are insects, spiders weaving webs with their bodies to trap us, their prey. I thought you were different. How could you fail to recognize my devotion to you?"

Peter's voice was filled with anguish. He was pleading, and his arms were spread wide in a gesture of total incomprehension. "Why did you fail me, Ruth?" His arms fell slack against his sides. He was suddenly limp.

Ruth's fear was so great she was sure it would have the power to move her. But try as she might, she was locked into her chair as surely as if she had been strapped in. She gazed in horror as Peter walked over to his cluttered desk, opened the right-hand drawer, and took out a double-headed ax. She recognized it as the twin of the ax that had killed her father.

Peter saw her eyes focus on the weapon.

"Yes, Ruth, I am the one who killed your father. I knew he was in Nick's office. He called and asked me to meet him there. Nick, he said, was in the dark room, which would give us a few moments to talk. He said he had something he wanted to discuss about *Homo jekyllensis*. I have no idea what it was, but I knew the situation was perfect. Two birds with one stone. Your father dead and Nick the obvious suspect.

"Your father deserved to die. He enjoyed what was rightfully mine. Your grandfather, the great Senator Wyndham, was an outright crook. He built his fortune by sabotaging my father's invention and ruining his life as well as mine. The Wyndham Institute is a product of fraud and deceit. It deserves to be blown up, and it will be blown up."

Peter ran his thumb over the blades of the double-ax.

"I had a soft spot for Nick, but he knew too much and he took you from me. All the others were bad, but Montoya and Tariq were the worst. Montoya, Mr. Man-About-Town-Drug-Smuggler, thought he was in control, but he would have been nothing without me. And Tariq, what an uptight fanatic! He thinks he's supporting a heroic cause, but in reality his actions are fuelled by personal rage. Wouldn't it surprise him to know that the person giving him his orders is none other than one Peter Ryan? Yes, Ruth, he killed Montoya because I told him to. The fool believed it was an Al-Qaeda directive and that Montoya knew of the plan to obliterate the Institute. Tariq was dumb enough to try and frame me. He dropped the cigarette, hoping the police would find it and trace it back to me. But Padrone picked it up instead, and you brought it here. That was very stupid of you, Ruth."

Ruth's eyelids flickered.

"Does that surprise you, Ruth? When Al-Qaeda contacted me, I jumped at the chance. The US government colluded with your grandfather in destroying my family.

"Are you afraid, Ruth?" he asked with a bitter smile. "Are you afraid? You of all people, afraid of me?

"Look, Ruth. Look at the handle. Those ancient craftsmen did their job perfectly. The symmetry of the blades is magnificent. And believe me, the blades are sharp.

"They were both efficient killings, Ruth. Your father's and Ricardo's. The ax and Tariq's knife performed as they should, and Tariq has had a lot of practice in the art of decapitation. Except for the blood. The blood ran like a river across their desks and onto the floor. It was like the rivers of blood in Iraq. Rivers and rivers of blood, smashed bodies, guts spilling out in the sand."

Peter raised the ax in both hands and swung it with such force that his body turned a full circle. He fell to the floor in a crouch, facing Ruth. The ax dangled between his knees.

"At first there was a way out. Drugs. The army knew it too. The top brass even arranged the drugs for us. And for a while drugs eased the nightmare. It did help. I can't say it didn't. It still does. Pot, heroin, coke, booze, women. It certainly helped. But not for long. It doesn't last. I knew *you* would save me, Ruth. From the nightmares." Peter dropped to his knees and held out the ax toward Ruth.

"I would have taken good care of you, Ruth. But you didn't see it. You went too far. You never looked at me when Nick was around. It was as if I hardly existed. I gave you too much time, and I suspect that Nick knew about the drugs."

Peter saw the startled look in Ruth's eyes.

"He tried to hide it by saying something about the fishy smell. But it was obvious that he knew I was using the lab here to make drugs. Maybe he was warning me. Maybe he was being a friend after all. But how could I be sure he wouldn't change his mind some day? It was so easy to make the stuff, Ruth. And it worked!"

Peter stopped suddenly and clambered to his feet. He lurched toward the laboratory table and picked up the cigarette butt.

Ruth watched as he walked slowly toward her, clutching the ax in one hand, the cigarette in the other. He waved the butt of the cigarette in front of her. It was so close she could smell the tobacco.

"This," he said, "is PCP. It's easy to make, child's play. But it's not for children. It works like nothing else to kill the memories. It gives you power and control. Fires up the imagination too. It's not for everyday use. Just when you really need it. Occasionally. Ricardo took care of the rest. Ricardo and I were in it together."

Peter stopped speaking and knelt in front of Ruth.

She could see the beads of perspiration on his forehead and running down his cheeks. The armpits of his shirt were damp with sweat. He threw himself forward and buried his head in her lap. The ax in his right hand dangled over the arm of the chair imprisoning her. She felt only fear and the inevitability of her own death. Images of her father, Nick, Joe, and her mother flashed through her mind. It seemed as if Peter would lie there forever.

Then he raised his head slowly until it was inches from her face. His expression was twisted with pain and hate. "It was so stupid of Ricardo, Ruth. So stupid to let you discover the heroin. And so stupid of Tariq to try to frame me. I thought they were smarter than that. But they were convinced they were so brilliant that they even fooled themselves. The egomaniacs.

"Montoya really thought he had me over a barrel for Samuel's murder. He saw me do it, you know. But he didn't realize who he was dealing with, did he Ruth? He thought he was invulnerable, but after I ordered Tariq to kill him, he wasn't, was he?"

Peter began to laugh, his face now contorted beyond recognition. "The silly bastard." Peter stared at Ruth and was quiet. He saw fear in her eyes and was disgusted by it. He grasped the arms of her chair and pushed himself to his feet.

"Poor Ruth. You're just like the others, after all." Her fear gave him energy. He stood before her. Now his face was a mask, expressionless and motionless. With his eyes riveted on Ruth's neck, he raised the ax very slowly above his head.

CHAPTER 33

Tuesday, November 23, 4:45 p.m.

The gunshot shattered the silence.

Peter felt a stab of excruciating pain. He looked up. Everything seemed to be happening in slow motion. He watched the ax as it flew out of his grip, curving in the air, followed by an arc of blood. His arms seemed to float down in front of him. He saw the ragged flesh where the fingers of his right hand had been. The blood ran down his elbow. He heard the shouting and felt the blow land squarely on his chin.

Red gave way to black.

CHAPTER 34

Ruth was awakened by the sound of someone entering her room. She was in Webster Pavilion, Room 205, of Lenox Hill Hospital. As the blurred figure approached, she felt a stab of panic. She stifled an impulse to scream and then recognized the arms embracing her.

"Ruth, my love. I was so afraid that Joe would be too late. If anything had happened to you ..." Nick's voice trailed off, muffled. Ruth felt warm tears on her cheeks. She held Nick tightly.

"I was completely helpless," he said. "There was nothing I could do from prison to save you. The judge released me this morning. You were still asleep. But I knew the whole story by yesterday. I thought it was too late, that Joe would arrive too late. I knew you were in terrible danger."

"It's all right now. I am still here," Ruth mumbled, glad to be awake and in Nick's arms.

"Is it all right if I come in now?" boomed the hearty voice of Joe Padrone from the doorway. "I've got a little surprise with me." Padrone covered the distance from the door to Ruth's bed in two giant steps.

"What've you got there, Joe?" Ruth asked. "I don't need anything now that you are both here."

"What a girl!" Padrone turned to Nick. "She's been hobnobbing with a madman and she can still dish out compliments." Padrone's expression grew serious.

"Thank God you're all right, Ruth. Just don't try to be too brave. You've been through a terrible ordeal, and you're bound to be in shock for a while." Padrone patted her cheek.

"And now," he continued, reverting to his jovial self, "time for a little celebration." Padrone heaved the scuffed leather briefcase he was carrying onto the foot of Ruth's bed. He opened the clasp, reached in, and pulled out a bottle of Veuve Clicquot and three plastic champagne glasses.

"Sorry about the glassware, but I don't think it will affect the taste."

"I'm glad you didn't bring beer," said Ruth. "From now on I'm sticking to wine and champagne. Thanks, Joe."

Padrone unwound the wire from the top of the bottle and eased out the cork. When the cork shot through the air, Nick was ready with a glass to catch the foaming champagne.

"Is anything the matter?" inquired a voice at the door.

Padrone took one look at the starched white uniform and sank to his knees on the far side of Ruth's bed, hiding the bottle behind his back.

"I heard a popping noise," said the nurse suspiciously. "You *do* know that alcoholic beverages are not allowed on the premises?"

"Of course, nurse." Nick was perched awkwardly on the edge of the bed, his hands behind him, clutching the half-filled glass.

"All right then." The nurse marched out of the room. The moment the door closed behind her, the three occupants of 205 burst into laughter.

"God, some mothers do have 'em," said Padrone, lumbering back to his feet and filling the glasses.

"To Ruth," Nick raised his glass. "To Ruth d'Abernon—that is, if you still like the idea." He looked so humble that Ruth smiled. Nick went on. "How would you like to attend the exhibition dinner as Mr. and Mrs. d'Abernon?"

"I'd like it, Nick. In fact, I'd love it."

"It's settled then," said Nick, giving Ruth a hug. "As long as Joe agrees to give away the bride and be best man at the same time."

"I'd like it, Nick," said Padrone mimicking Ruth. "In fact, I'd love it."

Ruth laughed. "Now that the simple matters have been taken care of," she said as leaned against her pillow and balanced her champagne glass on the covers, "I want to know about the more complicated ones. What made Joe come to the lab? How did you know something was wrong?"

"Ask Sir Galahad, here"—Padrone nodded toward Nick— "pieced the whole thing together, sitting in his little cell. A regular Hercule Poirot. I still think you're in the wrong profession."

"There is one good thing about jail, Ruth. You do have time to think *and* to read and listen."

"Thinking I understand. But how did reading and listening help?" Ruth sipped her champagne.

Nick noticed the color coming back into her cheeks and the sparkle in her eyes.

"Well," he said. "I just happened to be reading the 'good book' you advised me to read. I was so down in the dumps that I chose Oscar Wilde's *The Portrait of Dorian Gray*. I thought the story would match my mood."

Nick paced around the small room. "I reached the part in the story where Dorian Gray confronts his own portrait and compares his reflection in a mirror with the sinister face on the canvas. For some reason I thought of Peter, of the contrast between his baby-face appearance and his cynical attitude. And then I came to the scene where Dorian murders the artist who painted the portrait. He stabs him in the neck. Suddenly everything fell into place. I knew without any doubt that Peter had to be the murderer. And I knew that you, Ruth, were in terrible danger." Nick stopped short and grasped Ruth's hand.

"What fell into a pattern, Nick?" Padrone asked. "I admit Peter was odd, eccentric even, and he certainly had a baby face. But a cold-blooded killer? He seemed such a nice, harmless guy. A bit of a buffoon. Drank way too much. But he was never unpleasant, never difficult to deal with. What made you single him out?"

"It wasn't any one thing, Joe. It was a lot of things. And maybe they wouldn't have come together at all if I hadn't been forced to eat in the prison cafeteria. That was an ordeal. The food was awful and the ritual of the thing completely degrading. Lining up, marching in, the plastic trays, and plastic utensils—but no knife, not even a plastic one." Nick looked up, the memory etched on his face.

"The kind of trays with indentations separating the meat from the vegetables and potatoes. Like plates for babies. I could feel the hatred, resentment, and suspicion all around me. I just sat and listened. Listened mostly to the scraping of spoons and forks. But there were a few conversations, and I remember one in particular. Someone was talking about being busted for angel dust."

"I presume you mean PCP?" Padrone said.

"That's what—" Ruth began.

"Wait a minute, Ruth," Nick interrupted. "Joe hasn't heard this yet, though I gather you know all about it. Yes, Joe, angel dust, PCP, elephant dust, PeaCePill, hog, crystal, it has all kinds of names, so I learned, but they all seem to be variations of the same lethal drug. It was originally used to tranquilize elephants. You can just image what a drug used on elephants could do to people. Kills them, of course, if they take too much. With less, they suffer from delusions of power, paranoia, and think they're in control. The police have developed new ways to deal with people who have taken PCP. The old-fashioned hammerlock is no good. PCP addicts don't feel any pain. And they are very strong."

"So, what has all this got to do with Peter, Nick? Are you suggesting that he took PCP?" Padrone asked.

"I know he did, Joe. And I'm certain you'll find that the white powder in the cigarette butt is PCP. It explains everything. People have been known to commit violent crimes under the influence of PCP. And the way Peter killed Samuel was certainly violent. And I know Peter made PCP in the lab. It's not difficult, especially not for a reputable chemist from a place like the Wyndham Institute. All you need is rudimentary equipment and a few chemicals: piperidine, cyclohexanone, potassium or sodium cyanide, and phenyl grignard. The only item in the recipe that is difficult to get is piperidine. The Drug Administration has put in on their list of dangerous substances. But with Peter's credentials, connections, and background, he wouldn't have had any trouble getting it. All you need to make PCP is some simple chemistry and you have a white, odorless compound that looks like salt."

"But how did you know Peter was using the lab to make it?" Ruth asked Nick. "He told me you knew. But there were so many things in that lab that looked like salt or sugar. How could you tell?"

"It was the fishy smell, as I learned from my dinner companions in prison. Funny, they opened up when I began asking them to tell me about PCP. One of the things that piperidine smells like is fish, or sometimes ammonia.

"I was always struck by those smells in Peter's lab. I thought the fishy smell was because he was too lazy to clean out the fish tank often enough and that the ammonia was what the cleaning staff used for the lab floor. But I should have known that Peter loved his fish too much to neglect them." Nick paused.

"Go on," Padrone urged. "Take us to the end. I want to hear every detail."

"Well," Nick continued, "there was the time Montoya peered around the lab door and told Peter he had another shipment for him to unpack. I don't remember if you were there, Ruth."

Ruth shook her head.

"Anyway, the moment Montoya saw me, he disappeared. Said something about not wanting to disturb us. I was surprised, almost angry at that idiot." Nick caught himself. "Excuse me, *de mortuis nil nisi bonum*—not supposed to speak ill of the dead. I couldn't understand why Peter would unpack for Ricardo. We usually unpacked our own shipments of objects and then brought them to Peter for testing. But then after Ruth's escapade, excuse me, "adventure" with Ricardo, I got to thinking about the heroin. Then it became crystal clear. Peter must have unpacked the crates because Ricardo's objects were hollow on the inside and filled with heroin. He tested one and diluted the other. I always wondered why Peter had so much baby powder in the lab. I used to joke about his baby face. He brushed me off with a remark about showering and shaving when he spent the night at the lab. Of course he really used it to cut the heroin—a well-established practice, I gather.

"Which brings me to the last point: Peter's drinking. I think everyone at the Institute assumed Peter was a harmless alcoholic or maybe even just a heavy social drinker. His chronic lateness, perspiration, headaches, all pointed to alcoholism. I guess we overlooked it because he was so good at his job, such as it was. Not the most demanding work in the world for someone of Peter's intelligence, but he seemed to do it well enough, and he got along with everyone. In fact, I was fond of him myself. I attributed his peculiar behavior to his experiences in Iraq. But alcohol was not

Peter's main problem; it was the drugs. They were destroying his mind. I think he depended on them more than he thought. His deal with Ricardo began as a business arrangement and then became an addiction. Ricardo knew that Peter killed Samuel, Ruth."

Ruth nodded. "And I know why he did it."

"You do?" Nick and Padrone said in unison.

"Yes, he hated my father and grandfather. If you think about it, for all his talk, we knew very little about Peter. But he told me the whole story when he was about to kill me. His father was my grandfather's business partner early in his career, before he became a senator. Peter lived for revenge. He blamed my grandfather for sabotaging the patent that would have made his father a millionaire many times over and broken America's dependence on oil. He blamed my father for profiting from the fraud. He hated the Wyndhams, the US government, and the corrupt regimes in the Middle East. His hatred was so intense that he joined Al-Qaeda."

"My God!" exclaimed Padrone. "He seemed so genial."

"It certainly was an effective cover," said Nick. "He fooled us all."

"But how is all this connected with Ricardo? Why was he killed?" Padrone asked.

"He had to be," Nick explained.

"Ricardo was at his desk with his door open, and he had a clear view of who went in and out of my office. So he had to have seen Peter, and Peter had to silence him. But the question is how did Peter know that Samuel was in my office and that I was in the dark room?"

"I can explain that," said Ruth triumphantly. "Peter told me that my father had asked him to come up to Nick's office because he wanted to discuss something about *Homo jekyllensis*. He apparently wanted to tell Peter something before Nick was finished in the dark room. Peter didn't say what that was."

"I know what it was, Ruth. I haven't told anyone but Joe that your father made a mistake when he reconstructed the fragments of *Homo jekyllensis*. Carried away by his convictions, he falsified the reconstruction and combined fragments from two different skulls and skeletons, one *Homo sapiens,* the other Neanderthal. That's what we argued about. At first your father was furious, but his better judgment eventually prevailed, and he was coming to my office to discuss what could be done. I took his call in the dark room and told him that it would be ten minutes before I could safely turn on the lights and come out. That obviously provided Peter with the necessary time to kill Samuel."

Padrone interjected. "But Peter must have been high on PCP at the time and so fixated on his plan to kill Samuel that he didn't notice Ricardo. The problem with Ricardo was his arrogance. He considered Peter a buffoon and failed to appreciate how dangerous he was. He thought he could control Peter, but with drugs there is no controlling anything."

"It's funny you say that," Ruth shuddered. "That's exactly what Peter said."

"Ricardo certainly did underestimate Peter," continued Nick. "He may have been smart, but now it's clear that Peter was obsessed with a single goal: to kill Samuel Wyndham and destroy the Wyndham Institute."

"Peter did not kill Ricardo," Ruth interrupted. "Nadim did."

"How do you know?"

"Peter told me." Ruth repeated what Peter had said.

"You know, Ruth," Nick said, "as I think about it, Peter is a perfect example of your father's theory: part Jekyll, part Hyde, the isolation and aggression of Neanderthal combined with the intelligence and capacity for love of *Homo sapiens*. In fact, one might even go further and say that just about every curator at the Wyndham Institute illustrates Sam's belief in man's dual nature." Nick noticed the expressions of surprise that came over Joe and Ruth.

"Just think about it," Nick persisted. "Ricardo: cultivated, highly intelligent but the grandson of Nazis, a racist, and a drug dealer. Jorn: gifted and talented but split in two by his conflicting sexual inclinations. Lillian: the iron fist in a velvet glove. Even the genteel Dudley and grandmotherly Frances seem to have 'Neanderthal skeletons' in their respective closets.

"Not that I think your father would have been overjoyed to find his theories validated by his own curators, but who knows? As much as he loved, and lived for, the Institute, he was first and foremost a scholar and a thinker. I'm certain that's why he was so angry when I accused him of misleading the public, and perhaps even himself, about *Homo jekyllensis*. He was so sure of his theory that he couldn't wait for the evidence. He decided to help the conclusions along. I think that piece of scholarly deception preyed on him his entire life."

"Yes, I think it must have," Ruth agreed. "He was such a stickler for honesty in everything else."

"The worst part of it from that point of view," Nick went on, "is that his theory is now validated. *Homo sapiens* and Neanderthal man did interbreed. And I'm banking on his belief that the Neanderthal Factor in all of us can be controlled by culture and civilization. That's where I part company with Frances, who thinks our aggressive instinct is irremediable. But maybe Frances and I aren't really that far apart. It does all seem to boil down to the old debate about the relative importance of heredity versus environment, nature versus nurture. She stresses the first, while I emphasize the latter. Anyway, the first place in which I want to try and tame the Neanderthal Factor is in the Wyndham Institute.

"Well, it's over now, thank God. It really is over, Ruth." Nick stopped pacing and sat on the bed. He took Ruth's hands in his.

"You look tired. Joe and I should let you rest for a while. The nurse will be along any minute with your lunch. In fact, she's a bit late."

"I want to get out of here. I can rest just as well at home."

"Not before tomorrow. The doctor wants you under observation. You'll have to learn patience. After all, it's better than being in jail."

"I'm not so sure. But I guess one day won't kill me as long as you two come back later."

"It's not so bad," Padrone pointed out. "Even with that witch in white—" At that moment the door swung open and the nurse strode in carrying Ruth's lunch tray. She flashed Padrone an icy stare.

"Good-bye, Ruth." Padrone beat a hasty retreat past the starched figure. "Coming, Nick?" Padrone was out the door.

"In a minute. See you later, darling." Nick kissed Ruth and followed Joe.

"Judging from the look on the white witch's face, I would say that you are persona non grata around here, Joe. Or maybe she's hiding a soft spot for you."

Padrone grimaced.

"Let's go get some coffee. We have a lot to talk about."

"You're damned right we do, Mr. Director of the Wyndham Institute. The whole place needs an overhaul."

"Just what I was thinking. Where to begin?"

"With the Al-Qaeda cell run by Peter and his underling, Nadim. Not to mention the little surprise he planned for the exhibition dinner. You'll find there's another Neanderthal Factor for you. Tariq has the same overinflated ego as Montoya—thinks he's smarter than anyone else. But my security men aren't so dumb after all. "

"Joe, it's good to have you on my side."

EPILOGUE

R uth and Nick sat on the terrace of their hotel, sipping ice-cold raki, shielded from the hot sun under a green-and-white striped awning. They gazed across the Nile as they waited for the carriage that would take them from Luxor to the ruins of the temple at Karnak. The steamer that had brought them from Cairo two days previously was anchored a short distance up the river. It was visible from the terrace. Children played along the banks of the Nile as the sun shimmered across the water's surface.

An Egyptian picked his way among the terrace tables. He was selling four-day-old *Herald Tribunes*. Out of the corner of his eye, Nick glimpsed the headline. He signaled to the man.

"Look, Ruth." Nick pointed to the front page. "There's an article about the dinner at the Institute." He spread the paper flat on the table and began to read aloud.

EXHIBITION OPENING SPURS ISRAELI-ARAB AMITY

New York's Wyndham Institute was the scene of last night's dinner celebrating the opening of the exhibition on the Silk Road that was jointly sponsored with Cairo, Shanghai, Jerusalem, and the Wyndham Institute. The mayor of New York hosted the gala event. The presidents of Egypt and China and the prime minister of Israel were welcomed by Nicholas d'Abernon, the Institute's new director, and his wife, the former Ruth Wyndham. Mr. d'Abernon achieved notoriety recently when he was indicted for the murder of his father-in-law, Samuel P. Wyndham, the Institute's founder and late director. Mr. d'Abernon was subsequently acquitted of all charges and the Institute's chemist, Mr. Peter Ryan, is presently in custody and awaiting trial.

Because of the tense situation in the Middle East, the security precautions were elaborate.

"The press will never know just how elaborate!" exclaimed Nick, referring to the behind-the-scenes capture of Nadim and his hired assassin before they could carry out their plot and blow up the Wyndham Institute. The guests would never know how close to death they were that night. Fortunately, Padrone's plan had worked.

A waiter announced the arrival of their carriage. Nick folded up the *Tribune* and tucked in into his hip pocket. "Let's forget the Nadims of this world and enjoy the ruins of an old one." Nick reached for Ruth and pulled her up from her chair.

The carriage had seen better days. It was old and rickety, but the leather seat smelled of saddle soap and the fringes on the awning were tied with the same red and blue ribbons as the horse's mane. The old driver wore a flowing white djellaba and a red fez. As he helped the newlyweds into the carriage, he smiled and bowed.

Ruth noticed that his two front teeth were missing and that several others were gold.

When Ruth and Nick were settled, the driver jumped into his seat with surprising agility and cracked his whip. The horse trotted off at a brisk pace down the dry, dusty main street of Luxor toward Karnak.

"Happy?" Nick asked.

"Very. It was a wonderful idea to come here, away from the snow and cold. And from the Institute for a while."

The carriage wheels clattered along the cobblestoned Avenue of the Rams. The driver pulled to a stop outside the imposing facade of the Karnak temple.

Nick told the driver to return for them in three hours. He swung Ruth down from the carriage and they proceeded past the rows of ram-headed sphinxes lining the approach to the temple entrance.

The temple itself was an awesome sight and an extraordinary example of what the longing for life after death can inspire people to create. The structure was enormous, but it was only a small part of the much larger City of the Dead, the earthly residence of the Egyptian god Amon, which had taken nearly two thousand years to build.

Nick and Ruth strolled through the great Hypostyle Hall with its colossal columns, each rising to the sky like a giant, stylized lotus stalk. Neither spoke as they proceeded past the eerie shadows cast by the columns. The alien, animal-headed gods and hieroglyphic inscriptions all conveyed a vivid impression of daily life thousands of years ago in Egypt. Images of farmers, fishermen, cattle drivers, dancing girls, and musicians were in evidence, keeping the pharaoh in touch with their life even after death.

When the couple arrived at the colossal statue of the pharaoh with his arms crossed over his chest and his hands grasping the sacred symbols of divine kingship, Nick pointed to the little figure of the queen. She stood knee-high between his feet.

"The Egyptian view of women," he said. "What do you think of that?"

"Not much," Ruth replied. "Times certainly have changed, thank goodness."

"Oh, I don't know," mused Nick. "They haven't changed much

here. Come to think of it, it might be kind of nice. Wife always at your feet, pipe and slippers—ouch!"

Ruth stepped firmly on Nick's foot. "That's what I think about women at your feet," she said.

"Okay, okay. Forget I said it."

Later that afternoon, Ruth and Nick rested by the sacred lake. The sun was beginning to set and an early evening chill had settled in the air. Ruth pulled her cardigan around her shoulders. She and Nick watched the sun descend toward the horizon. The reds, purples, and oranges turned the endless blue of the daytime sky into a vibrant backdrop for the temples.

Reluctantly, Nick interrupted their reverie.

"We'd better start back. The sunsets don't last long here, and we don't want to be attacked by a pharaoh's ghost."

As they made their way slowly back to the entrance of the temple, they passed a group of tourists.

"I'm glad I didn't see Karnak that way," said Ruth. "Even if you are a male chauvinist."

"Come on, Ruth, let's get back to the hotel. I'm thinking of a cool bath, a gin and tonic, and you." He put his arm around Ruth. "Tomorrow we'll go down to the Valley of the Kings and visit the nearby, spectacular rock-cut temple of Hatshepsut. She was one of only four female pharaohs, and she built an enormous temple during her reign. Then you'll see what the Egyptian queens could do."